“Believe me, I know how the handle things if it gets tough.”

Again, he was quiet, then he leaned forward and brushed his thumb over her bottom lip. She couldn’t fight the shiver that stole through her, or the heat it left behind.

“Some day maybe you’ll believe me that you don’t always need to deal with the tough times alone.” Then he dropped his hand. “Go on up the stairs so I can tell Thelma you made it upstairs okay.”

She couldn’t really come up with a response to that, so she turned and did as he suggested. Unlocking the door, she looked down at Santini.

“You can go now.”

It was dark but she could see him smile, and knew those damned dimples were flashing at her. “As soon as you lock the door, I’ll be on my way.”

She didn’t even respond to that. She slipped through the door then shut it behind her.

“Goodnight, Joey,” he said, just loud enough to allow his voice to drift up to her. She didn’t respond. She couldn’t. She thought for sure he had planned on making a play for her, even if he just tried to kiss her. But he didn’t.

And now she wanted to know why—and that bothered her more than anything else.

She pushed away from the door and was about to go jump in the shower when she heard the whistling. And of course, it was *The Halls of Montezuma*. She rolled her eyes and chuckled to herself.

“Damn Marine.”

A
Santini Christmas

MELISSA SCHROEDER

ISBN:
1493579517
ISBN-13:
978-1493579518

DEDICATION

To the men and women of the military and their families. This time of year is specially hard to spent apart and I know you ache to be with your loved ones. Thank you for your dedication to our country and may we all have more peace on Earth.

Published by Harmless Publishing

Edited by Noel Varner
Cover by Brandy Walker

First print publication: November 2013

A Note from Mel:

Since I write a lot of contemporary novels, I am usually very careful about my hero and heroine practicing safe sex. But this book takes place in the 70's, long before the words safe sex really became buzz words for our culture. So, you will notice that condoms are not talked about here.

I also want to address the fact that date rape is discussed in the book. Again, this was not a term readily used or something that was even accepted as rape by many during the time of the book. I know that every person who experiences this violation and act of violence will have different reactions to it. Please know that my portrait of a surviving rape victim, especially in a time when people did not use the term date rape, is not flippant or glossing over the tragedy. The book is more about the woman she is now, than the woman she was then, and how it makes her view men in general. It does not diminish her experience or the tragedy that too many people suffer. Please know that this isn’t something I took lightly while writing the book.

Mel

CHAPTER ONE

Fear pumped through Joey Santini's body as she hurried down the hospital hallway. *Don't let him be dead.* It was a mantra she had said over and over since she'd gotten the call less than thirty minutes earlier. If she thought past that, Joey was pretty sure she would lose it. As she neared the ER doors, her phone rang with the Army Fight song.

Leo.

"Hey, Mom, where are you? I thought you and Dad would be here when we got in."

Shit. She forgot to call the kids. The three boys who lived outside of the DC area were all on their way into DC for the holiday. Great.

"I'm at the hospital," she said, making her way to the desk. She stopped by the door and waited to go in.

"What's going on?" Leo asked.

"Your father's been in a wreck. That's all I know."

She rushed through the doors and made her way to the information desk. "I'm Joey Santini. My husband is supposed to be here. Stewart Santini."

A young female attendant gave her an understanding smile. "Yes, ma'am. Let me check on his condition."

"What happened?" Leo asked, apparently ignoring the fact that she was trying to find out.

"I have no idea. I got the call not too long ago. I'm sorry I forgot to call everyone."

"Okay. Where are you?"

"I'm at Fauquier County Hospital."

"What happened?" he asked again. Somewhere in the back of her mind, she understood that he was confused and probably worried—not to mention she was the parent and she should be comforting him—but she didn't have the patience for that. Not now. Not since her world felt like it was falling apart.

"Listen, Leo, I don't have time for this. Call your brothers."

Then she hung up. She would pencil in time to feel guilty about that later. Right now, she could barely keep from passing out from the rush of panic she felt when she saw the clerk's grim expression.

"Mrs. Santini, your husband is up in surgery right now, but I understand they are almost done. Harold here will direct you to that floor."

She noticed a young man dressed in scrubs who was smiling at her in that understanding manner people used when there was bad news. Her heart sank. Just right there she had to keep herself from falling apart. Joey Santini didn't fall apart. Not in public.

"Mrs. Santini?" he asked gently.

She swallowed the knot in her throat, but it did nothing to help the way her stomach had soured.

"I can take you up to the surgery wing."

She couldn't speak. She was actually afraid to. Drawing in a deep breath, she nodded, then followed the young man to the elevators. Joey remembered stepping into the elevator, but the next few minutes seemed to pass in a whirl. She didn't truly remember the trip to the floor. She was in shock—that much she understood. She went through the motions. But she couldn't seem to make herself snap out of it.

They arrived on the floor and the young man led her to the long row of chairs that lined the hallway. The smell of antiseptic was even worse on this floor. It was so overpowering she almost gagged on it. She had always hated the scent.

He motioned toward the seats and said, "You stay right here. I will find out what is going on."

She didn't truly remember moving toward them and sitting down. Joey didn't know how long she sat there staring into space thinking that her life might have just ended. Without Stewart, she didn't want to think about tomorrow.

She felt someone touch her hand and she looked up. It was the attendant who looked a bit more relieved. The pressure in her chest eased a little.

"They're still working on him. The wreck left him with a

concussion and a compound fracture in his leg. That's what they are working on." He leaned forward. "I'm not supposed to tell you about that last part, but I couldn't leave you here worried about him."

Relief coursed through her, although she tried to keep it at bay. He was still in surgery and anything could go wrong. Tears burned the backs of her eyes. She blinked trying to keep them from falling. When she spoke, her voice caught. "Thank you."

"Do you need me to call anyone?"

It took her a moment to figure out he was trying to ask about family.

"Uh, no. I called them. Or…" She closed her eyes and drew in a deep breath reminding herself the young man said Stewart was okay. When she felt steadier, she opened her eyes. "I was on the phone with him when I walked in. They know where I am."

"You can call and give them an update, just make sure you do it in the hallway."

She nodded.

"Are you sure you're going to be okay?"

"Thank you, I'm fine."

He patted her hand and then straightened. "You remind me of my mother and I couldn't leave you here on your own."

She chuckled, albeit watery, but at least she chuckled. "That man in there," she said pointing toward the doors where the attendant had disappeared earlier "is a Marine. That makes me a Marine wife. I can handle anything."

Or she hoped she could handle it. For the first time since becoming that Marine wife, she wondered if she could. The elevator doors dinged open. Leo and MJ came rushing out, babies Anna and Serena in tow. Relief rushed through her. She didn't realize until that moment that she needed her family there.

"There's one of my boys. I'll be fine now."

He smiled down at her. "You take care."

He walked off as Leo and MJ walked up. Her second born looked tired but no more than any other new parent. His wife of less than two years, MJ, had been a perfect match for him in everything from their passion for their health care careers to their love for each other.

"Have you heard anything?" Leo asked, his brown eyes filled with worry as he rocked Serena in his arms.

MJ sighed and handed him Anna also. "Leo, really."

She leaned forward and gave Joey a hug. Joey could smell baby powder and formula. When MJ pulled back, Joey felt better. Her daughter-in-law's gaze moved over Joey. And even though she had just had twins less than six months earlier, she didn't look any different. Her long brown hair was up in a ponytail and her face was as fresh as on Leo and MJ's wedding day.

"How are you doing?" MJ asked.

"Fine, and for the record, your father is still in surgery. He has a compound fracture, so that is giving them some problems. Did you call your brothers?"

Leo nodded. “Well, I left a message for Marco because they’re still flying. Gee and Kianna are just past Charlotte, so they said to keep them updated. Vince is on his way over with Jules.”

She sighed. “I really hate to think of her out in this weather.”

Her daughter-in-law was newly pregnant, but having a rough time of it. Morning sickness kept her down most days.

Leo opened his mouth but the elevator doors opened again and a Fauquier County Officer came striding in. He zeroed in on her and headed over.

“Are you Josephina Santini?”

She nodded.

“I’m Officer Faison. I was on the scene of your husband’s wreck. It’s being investigated as a DUI incident.”

Anger and stress had her standing up, placing her hands on her hips and going toe to toe with the officer.

“I can assure you that my husband was not drinking.”

He actually took a step back and she realized she might have scared him. “No, not Mr. Santini. The other driver was drinking.”

“Oh.” Her anger dissolved and she felt strangely out of sorts. She had nowhere to

“Is he going to be okay?”

“Not sure yet. He’s in surgery right now.”

As soon as she said it, the doors at the other end of the hall opened and a tired looking woman in a pair of scrubs came walking out. She stopped at the nurses' station and the woman sitting there pointed toward Joey. The surgeon walked in their direction.

"Mrs. Santini?"

She nodded as she felt MJ slip an arm around her waist. It was a small thing, but feeling MJ's warmth bolstered Joey's resolve. She knew that her daughter-in-law understood better than her son.

"Your husband is going to be fine. He had some internal bleeding we had to get under control and we also set the fracture. He's going to have a long road with physical therapy, but he should be fine."

She closed her eyes and said a silent prayer of thanks. MJ squeezed her closer.

"Can I see him?" Joey asked happy that she didn't sound quite as pathetic as before.

"They should have him settled in his room soon. They'll come get you."

"Mom?" Vince asked from behind her. Her oldest strode down the hall like…well…a Marine. He dragged poor Jules behind him. "Is Dad okay?'

Joey nodded even as she had to keep blinking. If she didn't, there was a good chance she would start blubbering. Vince closed his eyes. When he opened them, she saw the relief she felt.

With a sigh, Joey walked over to the chair and collapsed. She couldn't cry yet. Not with her babies there and in front of everyone. That could come later. Just those few minutes had almost done her in.

She looked up and found both of her boys watching her with the oddest looks on their faces. Great, now they were worried about her. Joey figured it was because she wasn't yelling at everyone. She knew that for the boys, they worried when she got quiet.

Since she knew both of them were so much like their father, Joey decided to give them a task.

"Could someone get me a cup of coffee?"

"Sure," Vicente said as he led Jules over to the chair next to Joey's. Once he had his wife settled, he motioned with his head and Leo apparently picked up on it. "

"We'll be back," Leo said, leaning forward and giving her a kiss on the cheek.

Once they were finally man free, she smiled at MJ. "Now, give me those grandbabies."

"Are you sure?"

"Honey, I would much rather be holding life in my hands than worrying about the man in there."

* * * *

It took close to an hour before they were finally in the room with Stewart. He was sleeping and as the nurse said, he would mainly sleep through the day. They had him on some major drugs to help with the pain.

"You can go home, Mom. Leo and I can stay here."

She glanced at Vince then looked at Leo. "No. I'll stay. You two go back, take care of the babies and the women. When Gee and Marco get here, bring them in."

From the way Vince set his jaw, she knew he wanted to argue with her. Thankfully, Jules pulled on his arm. "Leave your mother with him. She'll let us know if anything goes wrong."

He hesitated, but Jules leaned closer and whispered in his ear, and Vince relented. "Okay, but I want updates."

She started to chuckle at the order. Her boys just didn't tell her what to do. But, instead, a sob broke free. Both of her boys froze. Jules stepped forward and put her arm around Joey.

"He is always trying to order people around like that. Your mother doesn't need that right now," she admonished. "Do you want anything to eat?'

The thought of food had bile rising in her throat. Joey knew she was still too unsettled to deal with that right now. She shook her head.

Jules smiled. "Let's go boys. We can grab MJ from the mother's room."

As they shuffled out, both of the boys gave her a kiss on the cheek. When she was finally alone, she settled in the chair next to Stewart and watched him sleep. He looked so tired, as if he hadn't slept in weeks, although she knew that wasn't true. He'd been beside her every night in bed. Dark circles marred the skin beneath his eyes. It had to be the wreck.

She sighed as she scooted closer, needing contact with him. She slipped her hand in his and brought it up to kiss his fingers. The tears she had been holding off came up and now she let them flow. It only lasted a minute or two. Then she dabbed her eyes and settled back in the uncomfortable chair, her hand in Stewart's, and drifted off to sleep.

CHAPTER TWO

Jacksonville, NC, 1975

Joey Antonio wanted to cut off her feet. Even with the comfy sneakers she wore, her soles ached. Sharp pain radiated through them all the way up her legs. Twelve hours at two different jobs was starting to get to her.

"You need a vacation," Sam said. She glanced at the bartender-owner of the Hideaway. He looked ready to fall over himself. Even his regularly cherry Hawaiian shirt did nothing to brighten his pallor. He was scraggly, not getting much sleep the last few weeks. And, she knew that this time of year was especially tough on him. They had a bad time of it lately with his wife's accident. In fact, in the last couple of weeks, he looked like he had aged about ten years.

"I need a lot of things," she said covering up her worry with a smile. "One of them is that order."

His weathered face split into a smile as he did her bidding. He knew what it was like to struggle. His attention was snagged by something over her shoulder. She knew he couldn't see that well without the glasses that he refused to wear unless he was driving.

"You got another table, honey. Do you want Thelma to take it?"

Sam's wife had been making noises about coming back to work, but since she'd broken her arm, neither Sam nor Joey would allow it. She was there, but in the back room and more than likely sleeping—although Thelma would never admit it. If Sam was offering up his wife, Joey assumed she looked like a freaking Mac truck hit her. When she glanced over her shoulder, she knew now why Sam offered Thelma up. A table full of jarheads. Normally, she could handle it, but Sam must have sensed that she was at the end of her rope today.

"No. I can take them."

She straightened her shoulders, then walked her way over to the table. Being where the bar was, and the fact that Sam was a retired Marine, they always had a lot of them in for drinks. She had gotten accustomed to handling them over the last few months, but it hadn't been easy.

Striding over to the table, she took stock of the group, as she always did. Four of them, all in their twenties. Not new Marines. They were a little older than the newly minted recruit.

All of them were built, like most Marines, but she could tell they were friends and not family...not outside of the Marines.

"Good evening. What can I get for you?"

The four of them immediately grew quiet and all of them smiled, except one. He looked...well stunned was the best way to put it. The others all seemed to be ready to charm her though. Great. She wasn't in the mood for Lotharios.

The blond spoke up first. He was taller than the rest, had a bunch of freckles scattered over his face...but she wasn't fooled. Most of the ones who looked so innocent were the worst—she had learned that early enough in life.

"Whatcha got on tap, darlin'?" he asked, his voice heavy with Texas twang.

She named off the beers and he picked one. The other two agreed but the fourth kept staring at her. Not in a creepy way. Instead he looked shocked as if she had horns growing out of her head. She wanted to ask him what the hell was his problem, but the longer he stared at her, the more self-conscious she became. It took every bit of her control not to reach up and mess with her hair.

It didn't help that he was gorgeous. He was definitely the most attractive of the group. Dark hair, chocolate brown eyes, and he had one of those strong jaws that attracted her.

Well, used to attract her. She pushed that thought away and decided to get on with the order.

"And you? Do you want anything?"

Blondie glanced at his friend and laughed. "Cat got your tongue, Papa?"

He didn't say anything to his friend, and she was starting to wonder if there was something wrong with him. "Papa?" she asked.

"One of his nicknames."

Like she didn't know they all had nicknames for each other and that some of them were horrible. At least this one could be said in public.

"So, would you like to order or should I bring whatever I feel like bringing you?"

Papa shook himself and then...a slow smile curled his lips. Dimples appeared and Joey felt the air back up in her lungs. She did her best to suppress the sigh that threatened to escape. He was attractive to begin with but he was lethal with that smile. She was suddenly hot all over.

"Whiskey, neat."

She nodded and turned to rush back to the bar. Sam was setting up the last of her other order.

"Three Buds and whiskey neat for that Papa fellow."

For a second, Sam stilled then grabbed his glasses off the shelf. After slipping them on, he peered over her shoulder. "I'll be damned. Papa Santini, get your lily white ass over here."

She heard a laugh and then the man approached from behind. Sam came from around the bar—something he rarely did—and pulled the Marine into a bear hug.

"Let me look at you. Lord, I can't believe you're already old enough to be a Marine."

He laughed. "Mom says the same thing."

"Could we get those drinks?" her customers yelled from the other table.

She grabbed her tray and headed off to the other table. By the time she returned, Papa and Sam were already exchanging memories of old times.

"So, Joey, this here is Stewart Santini. His father and I served together. I'm still trying to find out why he didn't call me before he came down here."

"I wanted to surprise you. Mom says to tell you that they'll be down after the holidays and I'm supposed to make sure Thelma is taking it easy."

"She is, thanks to Joey here. Looks after her as if she were her own mother."

Sam and Thelma had only one son, who had been killed in action three years earlier. Since her parents were off in some foreign country again saving the world, Joey had become attached to the older couple.

When Papa or Stewart, or whoever he was, looked at her again, she felt that same weird reaction as earlier. Her body went hot like an electrical spark and she felt breathless. Silly, but nothing she couldn't handle.

"Well, my mother thanks you. Ever since she heard about Thelma's accident, she's been worried."

"How are your brothers?" Sam asked.

Good lord, there were more of them. The thought that there were more of them at home like him was mind-boggling.

"All fine. Dave is finishing up at Annapolis next year. Tony and Adam are still in high school."

"Let me get you those drinks."

Sam hurried around the bar. Stewart really hadn't taken his attention away from her since he had looked at her a few moments earlier.

"So, Joey has to be short for something."

She heard the charm there, and she was honest enough with herself to know it made her want to blush. She just wasn't stupid enough to fall for it.

"Yeah, it is, *Stewart*."

He chuckled. "I should have made sure Sam knew not to call me by my real name."

She heard the front door squeak open and a few college students came in. "I'm going to assume you can get your own drink."

"Sure thing, *Joey*." He had emphasized her name, rolling his thick northeastern accent over it. She would not admit to anyone but herself that it sent a rush of need coursing through her.

Wanting distance from her disturbing reaction to the Marine, she hurried off to the college students. It really had been a long freaking day.

CHAPTER THREE

Papa watched Joey work the tables as he sipped on his whiskey. It was an easy thing to do. She walked with ease around the entire bar, keeping her patrons happy with a smile. He'd never seen a woman who could smile like she owned the world. Not like that. Every time he saw it, he lost his train of thought.

He paid no attention to the conversation around him. His friends were in a lively discussion about their night on the town. Well, what little town there was *here*. He'd lost interest the moment he'd seen Joey. Music was blaring on the jukebox and there was an argument over at the pool tables. He ignored it all. It was easy to do with the object of his attention being so interesting.

"Earth to Papa," Andrews said. He glanced at the Texan and realized his friend had been trying to get his attention for a while.

Papa sipped his whisky nonchalantly and asked, "What?"

"We were talking about hitting Scores later."

He made a non-committal sound when he heard Joey laugh at something one of the idiotic college boys said. Dammit, she was avoiding their table as if they had the plague. He knew why the college boys were flirting with her. Part of it was the job. Any young man getting served beer would flirt with a waitress. They always hoped to either get her phone number or free beer. Or both. The other part of it was the woman.

Tall and slender, she definitely demanded attention as she walked through the bar. There was something else about her, something that drew the eye toward her.

"Santini," Johnson said.

"What?"

He'd loved the sassy long ponytail that swung back and forth as she hurried around the bar. She wasn't overly flirty and he realized that maybe she didn't realize just how sexy she was. Natural beauty was always a turn on for him. He didn't go for a lot of makeup on a woman. Just not his thing. He also liked the fact she wasn't super skinny. Especially that full, round ass of hers. The way her bellbottom jeans hugged her curves was enough to make a man beg. Hell, the top she wore kept moving so he was playing peekaboo with her belly button.

"You're going to give her the creeps if you keep watching her like that."

He sighed and looked back at his buddies. The four of them had known each other at Annapolis, but not that well. Making it through training together had drawn them closer. The fact they all got stationed together at Camp LeJeune recently just added to that. Still, they made him feel old. They were all around the same age, give or take a year, but being the oldest of four boys made him look at things differently. And now that he had seen Joey, he didn't feel the need to head out to a strip joint.

"You can go on without me. I'm going to spend some time talking to Sam."

Johnson, a bruiser of a guy from Idaho, "God, we've lost our leader, men. He's all soft on a woman."

Papa didn't say anything. He knew they didn't understand, and explaining the Santini curse to them wasn't going to help. It would just make them mock him even more. As a Santini, he understood it well. When he had seen her, he'd felt like he'd had the air knocked out of him. After that, he didn't remember much.

"I told you Sam and my dad went way back."

The other shock of the evening was seeing just how old Sam had gotten. Papa's father had aged, but Sam…the years had weighed heavy on the Marine. Papa knew both Sam and Thelma had taken the death of Mike, their son, hard.

"Sure," Donaldson. "It has nothing to do with that fine filly that's been flitting around the tables."

Born and raised on a ranch in Montana, everything he said had to do with horses. Anyone else, Papa wouldn't like the term filly used for

Joey, but with Donaldson, it was nothing.

They finished off their beers and left him with the check, as usual, and headed out the door. Joey came up to collect their glasses. "Your friends abandon you?"

Again, he couldn't speak. Dammit, what the hell was wrong with him? Just like last time, it seemed his tongue was glued to the top of his mouth. This went beyond attraction, but he didn't even want to think about that.

Of course, he could come up with all kinds of other things he would like to think about. Like what it would be like to have Joey slip right there onto his lap and give him a kiss.

Then he realized she was looking at him waiting for his response to her question. Dammit, what had she asked him? Oh, his friends.

"Uh, yeah."

That will impress her, Santini.

"It was nice to see Sam so happy. He's been kind of off lately."

With Christmas approaching, it would mean one thing that would get Sam down. "It's getting close."

"To the anniversary of Mike's death." She nodded and he knew she understood. "Yes. Plus, with Thelma being hurt."

"How did that happen? My mom said she didn't have the whole story."

Joey sighed as she stretched out her back. "She was out on the bike in the rain. Sam's been on her about driving the Harley during bad weather, but she doesn't listen to him. Someone ran a red light; she had to swerve and lost control. The doctor said she was lucky only to have broken her arm."

"Are you telling tales on me, girlie?" Thelma said. He had to look past Joey then down to see the miniature woman who had been a second mother to him.

When he glanced at Joey, he saw her face turn pink as if she got caught being naughty. It made her even cuter. And sexier.

"No. I'm just telling Stewart that you were being bad and riding in the rain."

"You and Sam." Thelma shook her head and then looked at Papa. "Are you going to sit there and stare at me or are you going to come give me a hug?"

He smiled, and did as he was ordered. He pulled the diminutive woman into a hug, being careful of her arm. Again, though, the woman surprised him. From the moment he'd met her all those years ago, he'd been surprised by her strength. When he let her go she smiled at him.

"Little Stewey Santini, all grown up. And in Special Forces. Hard to believe you're the same boy who broke all my Christmas lights."

"He broke your Christmas lights?" Joey asked, as she wiped off a nearby table and cleaned up the empty glasses.

Great, now he knew Thelma would go to town on stories with an interested party.

"Yes. He was bored one day when we were stationed at Quantico together with his folks. We lived next door to each other at the time and your poor mother. She was not having an easy time of it with Dave, who was just a toddler. At that time, she must have been about four months along with Tony and sick as a dog still."

"Mom says that should have been the omen that Tony would be a pain in the ass."

Thelma laughed, as he knew she would. "Well, ain't that the truth. Either way, this one was about five years old."

"Lord, your mother had two kids under five and was expecting another one?" Joey asked.

"Ahh, the Santinis couldn't seem to keep their hands to themselves," Thelma said, making him want to kill the woman he thought of as a second mother. "Anyway, I walk out and find little Stewey smacking all the lights on the bushes with a big stick. Of course, when he saw me, he dropped the branch and started to run."

Joey snorted. "Fleeing the scene of a crime."

"We were all scared of Miss Thelma," he said very seriously.

Thelma belted out a laugh. "Well, that's because you should have been."

Joey opened her mouth to say something, but there was a shout from the most recent table of college boys.

“Duty calls,” Joey said, and started to make her way over to the table. He couldn’t help but admire the way her full, rounded hips swayed from side to side. Damn the woman was put together just the way he liked. Lately it seemed like so many women were on diets trying to become as thin as a beanpole. Joey had curves—and in all the right places.

“You better watch where you’re looking, boy. Sam will definitely tear you a new one if you think you’re going to play around with Joey.”

He felt his face heat as he glanced at Thelma. “Sorry. I can’t…”

He heard Joey laugh and he couldn’t stop from looking over to see what it was.

“Oh…so that’s the way of it?” Thelma said, tsking. “The Santini Curse strikes another generation.”

“What’s that supposed to mean?”

“Boy, when a man looks ready to beat another man up because he made a woman laugh…he’s hooked.”

He opened his mouth to argue, but Thelma shook her head and patted his arm. “Don’t even try to argue with me. Just know that you are going to fight to get that one to pay attention to you. She’s got too much on her plate.”

“How so?”

Thelma looked like she was going to answer him, then she shook her head. "Naw, I think you need to work to find out. Things come too easy for pretty boys like you. Why don't you come on over to the bar so Sam and I can tell horrible stories about your parents and brothers."

He chuckled and grabbed the whiskey he was still working on. "Sure."

He'd work the problem of Joey out later.

CHAPTER FOUR

Joey locked the door just as another loud burst of laughter sounded from the bar. She grimaced before turning around. Stewart...Papa...whoever he was, hadn't left all night. He'd spent his time reminiscing with Sam and Thelma. It was good to see her bosses so happy for a while, but she wanted the Marine gone. Away. So she wouldn't drool over him.

With reluctance, she made her way to the bar. Studying the trio, she wondered what the attraction was about. She'd been working at the bar for about two years and had never had an issue with Marines before. Sure, she was able to admit that she was attracted to the physique. What hot-blooded American girl wasn't? Add in the service before self, especially after the last few years, and she found most of them damned admirable. This one...he pulled at her. Every now and then she would find him watching her before he had a chance to look away and part of her was intrigued. Joey knew she shouldn't be. She'd learned her lesson several years ago about pretty men. They were smooth and shiny on the surface...to hide the fact they were monsters beneath.

Before the dark memories could pull her back into that nightmare, she pushed them away and started to wipe down the bar.

"Joey, sweetie, go on up to your room. You have an early day tomorrow," Sam said.

"I'm just wiping down the tables. You and Thelma have to drive home."

He shook his head. "Go on. Hey, Stew, why don't you walk Joey to her apartment?"

Apartment was a stretch. It was more of a studio above the bar. The Jacksons had allowed her to stay there and almost free of rent. If it hadn't been for that, she wasn't sure if she would have made it the last year.

"Uh, I can walk myself. Like I do every night."

And she didn't like the idea of the Marine walking her up to her apartment. But, apparently, he did. He was already off his stool and heading her way. Dammit. Butterflies erupted in her stomach. Not the kind that spelled trouble but the ones who fluttered at the anticipation of being with him. Alone.

What the hell was wrong with her?

"It's better to just go along with Sam and Thelma," he said with an understanding smile.

He was right. When she first met them, Joey had tried her best to keep the relationship professional, but Sam and Thelma adopted people. They had taken her on as a waitress and as a part of their family. Now, she couldn't imagine a day going by that she didn't talk to them.

"Give me a second."

He nodded and went to what she assumed was parade rest to wait for her. She untied her apron and headed back to the office. After the day she had, she really didn't need this kind of irritation. She was pulling out her tip money when Thelma slipped into the office.

"What's got you in such a bad mood?"

She sighed. She loved Thelma like a mother, but the woman drove her crazy at times. She knew right now Thelma wanted Joey to date Santini. It had been months since she had attempted the insanity of dating. She'd been so uncomfortable with the very safe accountant that she had decided to give up on all dating. The idea of going out with a big, hulking, pretty Marine left her unsettled.

"Nothing. I'm just tired."

Thelma knew better. Joey could tell just from the way the woman was eyeing her. Thankfully, though, Thelma knew not to push it.

"Okay. You need to take it easy every now and then, Josephina."

"I would love to, but I want to have the money to start school next semester. I want to be able to just work here and go to school. That's not going to happen if I start to take it easy."

The older woman nodded. "Yeah, of course."

She slipped her tips into her wallet, then stood. "There will be time for fun later on."

Thelma shook her head. "You're way too serious for someone so young."

"Of course I am. Someone around here needs to act like an adult."

Thelma barked out a laugh. Joey loved the sound of it. It was like a fog horn and loud as one. Some people might call it obnoxious. Joey found it comforting. She gave Thelma a kiss on the cheek.

"See ya tomorrow."

Then she slipped out of the office. It was best to pretend she had no idea what her employer was up to. If she confronted Thelma, she would just deny it and become sneakier.

When Joey returned to the bar, Santini was standing there waiting for her. Lord, he cut a fine figure. People could say whatever they wanted about Marines, they definitely knew how to keep in shape. She'd love to sculpt him. And that was odd enough because that wasn't her regular medium.

"He was afraid you slipped out the back," Sam said with a chuckle. Santini shot the older man a nasty look then turned back to her.

"Ready?"

"As I'll ever be. Night, Sam."

"Night, Joey."

They said nothing to each other as they walked out of the bar and into the night. It might be close to Christmas, but Jacksonville wasn't exactly a wintery place. They'd had a bit of a December heat wave of sorts, leaving the air heavier with humidity. The balmy night air refreshed her, at least enough to walk the few steps it took to get to her apartment.

"The answer is no."

He said nothing as they kept walking a few more steps; the only sound was their feet against the gravel.

Finally, he said, "I didn't ask anything. Yet."

She sighed. "I know Thelma means well and I've heard her mention the Santinis a time or two. Still, I don't date. I don't have time for it."

Joey sensed more than saw his nod, and then he said, "Doesn't mean I can't at least try."

Lord, a stubborn one. She really didn't need that right now. She was so close to getting enough money to make the commute back and forth to Greenville. Being distracted by Papa wasn't a good thing. It was better that she let him know exactly where they stood. When they reached the steps that led to her apartment, she stopped. Turning to face him, she looked him directly in the eye.

"I don't date. I don't have time."

He rocked back on his heels as he studied her. She wondered how much he could see of her feelings in the dim streetlight. As a woman with good reason to be wary of men, she realized she didn't feel any of her usual anxiety with him. She was relaxed. Well, as relaxed as she could feel with ten thousand butterflies fluttering in her stomach.

That was enough to worry her.

"What makes you think I want to date you?"

His face was completely void of all expression. She snorted, then started laughing. He joined in and the ball of worry that had been building in her stomach loosened.

"Then why did you walk me to my apartment? It's not like I haven't done it every night."

He cocked his head to one side. She didn't like the way he studied her. It was as if she were some kind of puzzle he wanted to assemble. Joey knew from experience a man like him would not be happy with the end product.

"This isn't the safest part of Jacksonville to walk around at night by yourself."

She sighed. "Don't worry, Santini. I can take care of myself."

"I bet you can."

Joey rolled her eyes. "And don't use that patronizing tone men use with women."

"I was not using a patronizing tone."

"Believe me, I know how the handle things if it gets tough."

Again, he was quiet, then he leaned forward and brushed his thumb over her bottom lip. She couldn't fight the shiver that stole through her, or the heat it left behind.

"Some day maybe you'll believe me that you don't always need to deal with the tough times alone." Then he dropped his hand. "Go on up the stairs so I can tell Thelma you made it upstairs okay."

She couldn't really come up with a response to that, so she turned and did as he suggested. Unlocking the door, she looked down at Santini.

"You can go now."

It was dark but she could see him smile, and knew those damned dimples were flashing at her. "As soon as you lock the door, I'll be on my way."

She didn't even respond to that. She slipped through the door then shut it behind her.

"Goodnight, Joey," he said, just loud enough to allow his voice to drift up to her. She didn't respond. She couldn't. She thought for sure he had planned on making a play for her, even if he just tried to kiss her. But he didn't.

And now she wanted to know why—and that bothered her more than anything else.

She pushed away from the door and was about to go jump in the shower when she heard the whistling. And of course, it was *The Halls of Montezuma*. She rolled her eyes and chuckled to herself.

"Damn Marine."

CHAPTER FIVE

Papa sat on the hood of his car as he watched Joey walk up the sidewalk from the bus stop. He knew that she had been at her other job that morning and afternoon. He had been able to pry that much loose from Thelma, even if she did keep most of what she knew about the waitress to herself.

Women. They always stuck together.

He liked watching her. A lot. More than he should feel comfortable with. In the last week he'd been into the bar every night, and he had yet to learn much more about her. Sure, he knew she worked two jobs and didn't seem to have a social life. He knew she was from the Seattle area. Maybe.

That was it.

It bothered him on a level he didn't understand that he couldn't seem to stop thinking about her. Just today in a briefing he'd lost track of what the commander had been saying because he kept thinking about the way she laughed.

As the colonel had griped him out, he had silently sworn not to go to the bar again.

Yet here he was, watching her stride up the sidewalk with that no nonsense way of hers. Damn, he found it sexy. He liked a woman who knew her own power—although, he had serious doubts she knew just how sexy she was. He hadn't planned on coming there, but he found himself on his way before he realized it.

"Lost again, Santini?" Joey asked, not slowing down as she passed by him. It was much better than being totally ignored, which is what she did the first three days. It was a sad day when a Santini sat around waiting on a woman to talk to him.

"Nope. Got off work early, was wondering if you wanted to grab something to eat."

"I have to work tonight."

"You have to work every night. At least this way you'll have some food in you."

She opened her mouth to argue with him. The women sure did love to argue for the sake of arguing.

He set his finger on her mouth. It was the first time he had touched her since the night he met her. The truth was, Papa hadn't been so sure he would be able to touch her and let her go. So, to save himself from embarrassment, he had kept his hands to himself. Even with just this simple touch, he yearned for more but he knew she wasn't ready.

"Why not have dinner with me? No strings, just food."

She looked down at his fingers, which looked a bit comical because it made her appear cross-eyed. He dropped his hand.

"Just food?" she asked, suspicion lacing her tone.

He really wanted to know if she didn't trust Marines or were all men lumped into the category. Which was completely out of character for him. If a woman gave him the back off vibe, he did. No questions asked. But with Joey, there was something there.

"Promise. Cross my heart."

She cocked her head as she studied him. "And hope to die?"

"Never, not when I can have dinner with a woman like you."

Her sigh was long and filled with irritation, but apparently she'd decided to take a chance. "As long as you understand this is only dinner.

He smiled, knowing he had won at least this one battle. "Of course, if you feel the need to throw yourself at me, I will sacrifice myself. It's the least I can do."

Joey shook her head, her ponytail swinging back and forth behind her. "Give me a second. I'll be right back."

She jogged up the stairs and he leaned back against his car again. Today was shaping up to be a much better day than he expected.

* * * *

He let her pick the place, which made Joey happy. It made sense since she had lived there longer than he had, but men didn't always use good sense.

She suggested her favorite pizzeria and he hadn't batted an eye. She had expected him to say something but he didn't. He did sniff at the air as they were led to their table. Before they sat down, his lips curved.

"What?" she asked when the waitress had left them.

"Smells good. I can usually tell a good pizza place from the smells."

"How about I know my pizza."

He shrugged as he looked over the one page menu. "I don't know that much about you other than you work too hard and you're gorgeous."

For a second she just stared at him. In all her years, she had never really been called gorgeous. She'd been a skinny girl with a penchant for art and books. She hadn't fit into any group, really, being the daughter of missionaries who often left her for their work.

She leaned across the table. "You know you don't have to keep up the charade, Santini."

He glanced up at her and every thought in her head seemed to evaporate. He had an amazing set of eyes. She had described them as chocolate brown, but that didn't do them justice. A small line of gold rimmed his iris and sometimes, when the sun hit them just right, she could see shades of green within them. They seemed to always change their shade and, for an artist, it held her mesmerized.

"What charade would that be, Joey?"

God, the way he said her name. It made her all squishy on the inside. Worse, it made her want to reach across the table and pull him closer for a long, wet kiss.

Fudge.

"That you're interested in me. You don't have to try and romance me because there will be no romance. I don't have time for it or for you."

Pretending to be more interested in her menu, she picked it up off the table and blocked out the sight of him. It only took a couple of seconds before she felt a tug on the top of the menu. She looked up and found Santini looking over the edge of the laminated paper.

"Everyone needs a little romance."

"I know that as a Marine, you're only out for a good time. That's great. But I only have time for work. Then, next semester, school."

He nodded and looked at his menu again. "Sure. I get that. Not like I'm busy or anything protecting the world."

She heard the sarcasm in his voice and couldn't fight the chuckle that bubbled out. He looked at her and smiled the slow sexy smile that she already loved.

"You should laugh more often. It's a really pretty sound."

She said nothing to that and thanked the good lord the waitress returned with their drinks. "Do you know what you want?"

"Want me to order?" he asked. "You know, being the Italian."

"You're not the only Italian at this table and I used to work in a pizzeria. Anything without peppers or anchovies is fine by me."

As soon as he ordered, and the waitress left them alone, he kept staring at her.

"What?"

"Nothing. Nice to know you're Italian though."

"So I passed some kind of test by accident of birth?"

For a second he didn't say anything, then he laughed.

"What?"

"You have just the right amount of sarcasm to please me, Joey." He took a sip of his soda. "So, are you going to tell me your full first name?"

"You couldn't charm it out of Thelma?"

"No. She told me if you didn't want me to know, I didn't need to know."

She bit her bottom lip and tried to keep from laughing, but it was no use. He sounded so irritated by the whole issue. His eyes narrowed when she snorted.

"What?"

"So...poor little Marine couldn't get Thelma to tell him stuff?"

He made a face and she had to bite her lip to keep from laughing. He looked so put out.

“It didn’t used to be a problem.”

“I bet it’s never a problem for you.”

“What the hell is that supposed to mean?”

She realized then that she said it aloud. With a sigh, she decided to end any chance she had with the man—not that she wanted one.

“Listen, I get it. You’re big and tough, not to mention you’re a Marine and gorgeous. Women are always falling over themselves to get your attention. I’m sure that Thelma’s reaction to you is rooted in your time together when you were a little boy, but I am almost positive you were probably a pretty little boy too.”

He blinked, calling attention to those large dark lashes and those impossible milk chocolate eyes. “You think I’m gorgeous?”

Of course, out of all of that, that is the one thing he remembered.

She shrugged. “You don’t make me want to vomit when I see you.”

There was another beat of silence and she fiddled with the edge of the sleeve of her jean jacket.

“Well, that’s a good thing.”

He said it with enough self-depreciating humor that she had to smile. When she looked up from the table, she found him grinning at her.

"It is a good thing. I would have never been able to suggest pizza otherwise." He just kept grinning at her and there was a part of her that wanted to go with the flow. There was no way there would be anything between them. She didn't know when she would trust a man that much again. Since he was a Marine who would probably ship out at some point, there was no reason to think there would be anything between them.

"Listen—"

"Oh, that doesn't sound good," he said easily.

She sighed. "I don't date for a good reason. I don't have time." That sounded good. It was at least partially true.

"Really?"

He sounded skeptical but not sarcastic. There was at least that.

"Yes. I am trying to save up some money for school."

"Your folks can't help?'

She shook her head. "No. They've got enough on their hands at the moment." Her father's illness wasn't something to talk about or the fact that when they did have money, her parents usually gave it away to those who needed it more.

He nodded. "I'm not sure if I would have made it through without going to Annapolis."

Of course, he was an Annapolis graduate. Then it dawned on her that he was a captain or O-3. There was a good chance he had been to

Vietnam before coming there.

"You've been in country?"

He nodded. "Just for six months though."

"And your brothers, none of them went?

He shook his head. "They all wanted to go. Mom was happy they didn't. She doesn't like her babies far from home."

She rolled her eyes. "Your poor mother having to deal with four boys. I wouldn't wish that on anyone."

He opened his mouth to say something but was interrupted by the server bringing them the pizza. When they were finally alone, she asked, "What?"

He shook his head. "I just never thought about how being a mom of four boys would deal with it. I guess my mom just never really showed that it bothered her much. Of course, she is kind of the rock star of the family."

"Oh, so a mama's boy?"

He blinked again, then he laughed out loud. "I can't win with you. But no, I am not the mama's boy. That's Adam. He's the youngest and he's been babied his whole life."

"And I bet you and your other brothers made his life hell."

"It was our duty as older brothers."

She grabbed a piece of pizza and bit into it. The moment the hot cheese hit her mouth she realized how hungry she was. It had been seven hours since she had last eaten. Joey hummed as the cheese and pizza sauce danced over her taste buds.

She didn't realize that Stewart had stopped eating to look at her and then she realized how loud her moan had been. Her face heated with embarrassment.

"Sorry. It's been a long time since I've had a piece of pizza."

He said nothing to that as she took another bite. There were times he would just watch her, as if trying to figure her out. It always made her nervous.

"So, you really don't get out?" he asked.

"I work over sixty hours a week. What do you think?"

"Yeah, I get that, but I would think now and then you'd have a date."

That was tricky territory for her. She had her reasons for not dating. Most people didn't believe her or thought she was insane.

"I don't have the time or inclination. And while working at the bar gives me lots of choices, they aren't that great."

"And your daytime job?"

"What about it?"

"Well, are there any men there you might be in contact with?"

He asked it so casually she realized he was trying his best to keep it light, but he was definitely feeling her out to see if she was seeing someone else.

"No. Definitely not."

"Still not going to tell me what you do during the day?"

"You've never asked me." She knew she was pushing his buttons. Marines liked to be in control of the situation and he really didn't like that she had power over him.

"What do you do during the day?"

"I work at that strip joint a couple streets over."

Joey was proud of herself for keeping a straight face when she said it. His gaze shot up to hers then he laughed.

"You definitely have a smart mouth."

She shrugged. "Better than a stupid one."

He chuckled. "Okay, so, what do you really do?"

"I work at an art supply shop. Really, a hobby kind of shop where they have toy models and stuff to put together. I'm in charge of the paint area, plus I teach art classes to kids."

"You know about model airplanes?"

"I do now, but I took the job to get the discount on paint supplies."

"You paint?"

"Yes. That's what I'm saving my money for. Art school."

She waited for him to change the subject. Most men did. Hell, most people did when she started talking art. They would rather pretend she wasn't some kind of hippy painter. She knew her parents would have been happy to pretend she wasn't going to pursue a career in painting.

"That's pretty cool. So, what kinds of things do you like to paint?"

Joey didn't answer that question. Irritation with him, with herself for "Why are you doing this?"

"Doing what?"

"You really want to know about my painting?"

"Yeah. I do."

He said it so naturally, she believed him. There had been no hesitation and his gaze was sincere.

"Why?"

"Because it has to do with you."

Again, so simple to him and she relaxed.

"I like to do mainly oils and landscapes, but not a lot of portraits except of people I care about. I have a lot to learn though. I have always wanted to try sculpting, but never have. Not seriously."

And then she sat back and studied Stewart. He would be a perfect model in any medium. Of course, sculpting would be best. She hadn't seen him with his shirt off, but she could imagine the sculpted muscle beneath the olive toned flesh.

"Earth to Joey," he said, his tone filled with amusement.

Joey blinked then refocused on this face. From his expression she could tell he knew what she had been thinking. Her face heated and she tried to pretend she didn't know why he was amused.

"You want to talk about it?"

"There's nothing to talk about, Santini."

He sighed. "Now I know I irritated you. You use my last name when you're irritated with me."

But in her head she used his first name.

"So, that's why I always call you Santini."

He chuckled. "At least you're thinking about me."

It would be better to change the subject and just move on from the dangerous topic of her liking him or that she thought about him…and his muscles.

"So, what do you do in your job?"

He smiled.

"What?"

"Women usually don't ask about that. Not really. Not like they really want to know."

"But I do." And as soon as she said it, she realized she really did. She might not want a romance with the Marine, but she did like him. In a totally platonic way. Like a brother with a really sexy smile.

"I'm Force Recon."

"That means?"

"We would go out on search parties, look for the bad guys."

And there was more to it than that, but he wasn't going to say it. She could tell by his expression that his one time in country hadn't been that easy.

"So, do you think you like me enough to buy me a cannoli?"

He looked at her for a second or two, then he threw his head back and laughed. After a few moments, he quieted.

"Listen, Joey, there isn't much I wouldn't do for you, and I'll definitely buy you a cannoli."

CHAPTER SIX

Papa fought the need to wipe his palms against his jeans. He hadn't been this nervous taking a girl home since his first date. And this wasn't even a real date. Just two friends grabbing a bite to eat.

"So, I assume you're working until closing tonight."

She glanced at him then away. "Yeah. I work almost every night."

"I should have a talk with Sam about working you so hard."

She snorted. "Sam does it out of the kindness of his heart. I need the hours and tips."

"What do you mean by that?"

"You know Sam and Thelma could handle most nights there by themselves. They don't really need me on the weekday nights, but they both know I need the money."

A gust of wind rushed over the two of them and he watched as her ponytail danced. He'd become obsessed with her ponytail. Not since he'd been in junior high had he been this consumed with touching a girl's hair.

Sad, Santini. Really sad.

They turned the corner and her apartment came into view.

"How did you ever meet them?"

It was a legitimate question. This wasn't a place where a lot of locals would hang. It was more for military and those college kids who wandered into town to enjoy the beach.

Her mouth curved. "They came into where I worked at the time. It was this horrible bar and grill. It was upscale but my boss was the worst. That night, things went wrong, just really wrong. It ended up with me punching him the nose."

He stopped walking and just stared at her. She wasn't a big woman. In fact, with her small bone structure, she was downright tiny. He sometimes forgot that because of her personality. She was…well, bigger than life most of the time.

She stopped and looked at him.

"What's up?"

"Just hard to see you hit someone."

She laughed, a real laugh. It floated over the cool December air to him. His palms started to sweat again.

"You would have thought a man that big wouldn't go down so easily, but I hit him square in the nose. The crunch of bone was disgusting. I think it was more the sight of his own blood that made him pass out." Joey leaned against the building of her apartment and sighed. "I don't feel like going to work tonight."

"Then don't."

She smiled. "I have to. Thanks for dinner."

He placed a hand on the wall beside her head and gave into that need, the one that had been keeping him up at nights and turning down his friends' invitations for debauchery. He didn't want that. Didn't need it. He had Joey.

She was so delighted with herself, her joy so easy to see, that he couldn't stop from leaning forward and brushing his mouth against hers. He hadn't touched her since the first night he met her. He wanted to devour her there, just lose himself in the taste of her. But he couldn't. There was something that told him she didn't have much experience and he didn't want to push her.

So, before he was ready, he pulled back. Her eyes were wide with an emotion he couldn't discern. Maybe he didn't want to.

"You're very welcome."

She nodded, then without another word, slipped away and walked up the stairs to her apartment.

He'd planned on going back to the base, but maybe, he'd hang out at the bar tonight.

* * * *

Joey dropped another glass. At least this one didn't break. It was the fourth one tonight. If she wasn't careful, Sam might start charging her for them.

"You seem to have your mind on other things," Sam said.

"Just tired."

That sounded right. It wasn't, but anyone would be tired if they were on hour sixteen of work. Add in a sexy Marine clouding her judgment, most people would understand. Still, she didn't want to admit it to the man she thought of as a second father.

"Go, then, you need some rest."

She wished it was the simple. A good night of sleep had been eluding her since she'd met Stewart. Every time they met up, it got worse. And the most devastating thing was that she wanted to paint him.

She heard him laugh across the room and she shivered. Not that she was cold. Sneaking a peek, she saw he was over in the corner with Thelma again. That was one thing she was thankful for. Stewart had kept Thelma out of the way and resting that arm of hers. Her employer probably didn't realize she was getting the cast off tomorrow. Stewart had kept Thelma occupied during their busy times. Joey knew Sam had been grateful.

There was a kindness about him that got to her. She saw it every day and not just with her and Thelma. She saw the way he talked to some of the old timers who wanted to talk of their days in the Marines. He showed amazing patience with them and they were some of her favorite customers.

"Joey?"

She shook herself when she realized that Sam had said her name several times.

"Sorry. I guess I was day dreaming."

She looked at the glasses on the bar. All of the sudden, Joey realized Sam had gotten her order ready and had been waiting for her to put it on the tray and take it out. She did that and made her way back to the bar.

"Are you sure you're alright?" Sam asked.

When she glanced up from adding up the bill for one table ready to leave, she noticed he wasn't kidding like he normally was. Sam was seldom serious and when he was, she took notice.

"Yes. I've been busy."

"Yeah, I know you have. If you don't like Papa bothering you, let me know. I'll have a chat with him."

Joey had told Thelma of her rape in high school. It had been the worst night of her life and every now and then, it came back to her. She'd had a reaction to one of their customers and Thelma had realized the situation. Before she knew what was happening, Joey was pouring her heart out to Thelma. From what Joey knew of their relationship, she was pretty sure Thelma probably told Sam.

She shook her head. "No. He has been a perfect gentleman."

Sam sighed. "How about you take tomorrow night off? You know once Thelma gets that cast off, she's going to want to be out and about with the customers."

Normally, she would panic because of the loss of tip money, but it had been a good few weeks. Christmas was usually a good time to work in a bar, at least at the Hideaway.

"Sounds good."

"What sounds so good?" Thelma asked. She'd walked up to the bar with Stewart.

"I said Joey here needs a night off."

Thelma nodded. "I agree. In fact, you really need a night out on the town."

"What I need is a night of sleeping," she said with a laugh.

"Now, you are too young for that." Thelma looked at Stewart. "You need to take the girl out."

Stewart chuckled. "I think I can get my own dates, Thelma."

"Oh, come now, Stewie, you know you had a time of it with that...what was her name?"

At first, Joey had wanted to escape until she saw the flush in Stewart's cheeks, she had to stick around.

"I have no idea what you're talking about," he mumbled.

Thelma rolled her eyes. "You know, Sam, that major's daughter. Real piece of work she was. Betty Sue...dammit what was her name?"

"Bethany and she wasn't a piece of work," Stewart said.

Thelma ignored him. "So, it took him weeks to ask her out to the prom. You would have never thought he would. When he finally does get the nerve, she agrees and breaks up with that one kid. Wasn't a brat."

Meaning, he wasn't a military kid.

"So, what happened?" she asked, unable to ignore Stewart's discomfort.

"Nothing."

Thelma cackled. "Well, nothing to a Santini. The other boy was so upset that he tried to fight him after school. Got a broken jaw thanks to Stewie here."

"That's nothing to be proud of," Stewart said. Joey looked at him and realized he was being serious. He might be a warrior but he was one who understood that fighting should be your last resort.

Someone shouted Thelma's name and she went over to talk to friends. Sam was busy working the bar.

"So, what do you think about tomorrow night?" Stewart asked her.

"Are you asking me on a date?"

He hesitated then nodded. He looked so cute, his hands in his pockets as if he was trying to control himself. This big, bad Marine who hunted down people for a living was standing there like a teenager trying to ask a girl on his first date. It was funny and sweet at the same time. And for once, Joey decided to take a chance.

“Okay.”

His mouth opened, but no sound came out. He snapped it shut a moment later.

“Is there something wrong?” she asked when he still said nothing. He just kept staring at her.

He shook his head, keeping his gaze locked with hers.

There was a shout from the folks who had wanted to close out their tab. “I need to take care of this.”

“Is six-thirty too early?”

“Nope.”

“I’ll pick you up then.”

She nodded, unable to fight the smile that curved her lips. It might not be the smartest thing, but at least she knew she would have a fun time.

CHAPTER SEVEN

Papa watched the way the streetlights played over Joey's blonde hair. She had worn it down for their first real date and he hadn't realized how much he had wanted to see it dripping over her shoulders. He knew from touching it the night before when he kissed her that it was as soft as it looked, and thick. The only thing he could think about all night long was how it would feel against his bare flesh as he fell asleep.

"Are you planning on going home for Christmas?" she asked.

"No. Not much leave. I took off some time before coming here."

It wasn't exactly a lie. He could get home if he wanted to, but at the moment, it didn't seem that important. His mother had been disappointed. Still, there was something in her tone that told him Thelma had called and tattled on him. If he showed up for Christmas without Joey with him, there would be inquiries.

He shrugged that idea away and decided to worry about it later. Right now, he wasn't ready to give up what little headway he had made with Joey. He had finally talked her into dinner out...as in making plans ahead of time. He had wanted to kill his mother's friend when she told the story of Bethany Lewis, but he knew that had been part of what had won Joey over.

"I don't know when I had steak last," she said, breaking into his thoughts.

She kept saying things that intrigued him in different ways. Her past wasn't open for discussion. He got that from the first night he met her. He craved to know more. Papa hated to admit that he hadn't spent that much time getting to know a lot of the women he dated. He knew them...but not like he wanted to understand what made Joey act the way she did. When she spoke of art, she held nothing back.

"It's been a while for me too. I'm glad you suggested this place. I would have never guessed it was so good."

She shook her head. "If you're going to spend your life in the military, Santini, you need to experience the place you're at. I always think it's a shame that more people don't get out beyond that front gate."

"I think a lot of us are wary. At least the guys with families. The last few years haven't been the best for us."

She nodded in understanding. In his experience, a woman in Joey's position knew enough about her customers to do her job. He understood flirting was part of it. Tips helped a lot of them pay the bills. With Joey, though, she seemed to really care about the folks from the base. He'd seen her talk to guys, asking them about their families and girlfriends.

"So, will it be another month before you have a night off?"

She didn't say anything for a few seconds. "I don't get a lot of nights to myself. Of course, I like it that way."

They were standing at the base of the stairs to her apartment. He wanted more than anything to follow her up the stairs and spend the night. Papa wasn't sure how much experience she had, but he knew it wasn't much. He was pretty sure some bastard had hurt her in a way that made it hard for any guy to get her to go out…let alone share her bed.

"I take it you're not going home for Christmas?" he asked. He knew it was stupid because he already knew she was working at the bar. Papa was man enough to admit when he was desperate. He didn't want the date to end, not now, not ever.

"No. Working on Christmas Eve and then going to Sam and Thelma's for Christmas dinner."

He nodded, not telling her they were spending Christmas together. Thelma had said something about it earlier, sort of an assumption he would be at her house. It was a definite if Joey was there.

"I'm glad you finally came out with me."

"I've been out with you before, Santini."

He chuckled. "Grabbing a piece of pizza or taking a thirty minute walk on the beach is not a date."

She tilted her head to one side and studied him. He knew she was going to screw with him. Sadly, he was excited by even that.

"This was a date?"

He laughed, enjoying her. She had a wicked sense of humor. She laughed with him and he couldn't resist. He leaned forward and kissed her. She stopped laughing and stilled. Worried that he might have overstepped his bounds, he almost pulled back from her. In that next instant, she returned the kiss. Tentatively and with little skill. It was the sweetest and sexiest thing he had ever experienced.

Heat blasted through him, racing in his blood and soon, he wanted more. He needed that flesh-to-flesh contact. Knowing it was his only option; he cupped her face with one hand as he continued to kiss her. When he knew he was close to begging for an invitation upstairs, he pulled completely back. Then, he stepped away.

"Thank you for the date."

His voice was hoarse and it was worse that she looked as stunned as he felt. He hadn't had a kiss affect him that way before.

"You're welcome." She turned and practically ran up the stairs.

He shoved his hands into his pockets, waiting. When he heard the deadbolt slam home, he walked to his car. He could meet the guys out tonight, but he felt like a drive—then probably a cold shower.

One day, he promised himself, he would be snuggled up to the sexy waitress.

* * * *

"So, angel, when are you going to give up this life of hard work and become my lady?" one very annoying college kid asked Joey.

She didn't roll her eyes but it was close. She hated the last few days before Christmas. It seemed like every annoying frat boy made a stop in Jacksonville on his way home. And they always left horrible tips. She could handle Marines because most of them would tip her well for her troubles.

"Gee, I don't know about that. " It was about all she could muster. She was tired and cranky and she couldn't think straight most of the night. She'd been thinking more and more of going back to see her parents on the West Coast. She knew part of it was the season. She always grew homesick this time of year. The other part of it...well, she was being a coward. The last month Stewart had been getting under her skin. The few kisses they had shared hadn't scared her as much as the one from the night before had. That one hadn't just made her melt. She had yearned for more. She almost asked him up to her apartment. Just a kiss and Stewart almost had her. *Dammit.* She needed to start thinking of him as Santini. That would make him not a man. Just a Marine. A very sexy Marine who kissed her until she melted.

"Hey, did you hear what I said?"

The annoying college student asked the question and tugged on her arm. She almost lost her tray full of glasses.

"Sorry, it's hard to hear in here."

He still had hold of her arm and she sensed some kind of movement behind her. She knew without looking who was there.

"Is there a problem here?" Stewart asked, his voice deathly calm. She didn't think she'd ever heard that tone from him before.

The college kid's attention shifted from her to the hulking figure of Stewart. The sneer on his lips faded and he lost most of the color of his face.

"Uh..."

"Is that supposed to explain why you still have hold of the lady's arm?"

Frat boy looked down at her arm and then dropped it as if he had been burned.

"Sorry," he mumbled.

"I think you need to finish up and head on out."

"Yes, sir."

He sat back down and she turned to face Stewart. She wanted to tell him to take a leap, but the look on his face sent a blast of ice racing through her blood. This was not the man who had blushed when Thelma had told stories about him or the one who had kissed her the night before.

This was the Marine.

It took her another moment to gather her wits.

"Santini, take a step back."

He finally broke eye contact with the college kid. It took a second before his eyes softened a bit.

"Okay."

She stepped around him, but she felt him follow her back to the bar.

"Do you get that a lot?"

She didn't appreciate the tone. It was as if he was accusing her of something.

"Only when they drink too much. Of course, it isn't always college kids. I get problems from some of the Marines around here too. Drunkards come in all classes."

"What are their names?"

She glanced at him with a smile, realizing then that he was serious. "I don't know, Santini. I don't keep a record of every jackass that comes in here."

"You shouldn't have to deal with them."

Sam looked over at them, and moved away. Coward. He was abandoning her to Stewart's questions.

"I can deal with them."

He watched her in silence. She knew he wasn't done. She could practically feel his brooding. The man would have been a perfect

Bronte hero.

"Why do you work in a place like this?"

Irritation, lack of sleep, and her own homesickness had left her with little patience. She also didn't like that Stewart seemed to think he had a right to question her choices in life.

"I work here because I like Sam and Thelma. I also like most of the regulars."

"Well, you shouldn't."

She stopped putting the order Sam had just placed on the bar onto her tray.

"I don't think I asked for your opinion. In fact, it isn't any of your business."

She finished collecting the order and headed back out. It was loud and smoky and she was now getting a headache. She smiled and tried her best to work the tables like she normally did, but Stewart's attitude was starting to get her down. Worse, she couldn't argue with him any more when she returned to the bar because he was gone. Disappeared in the night apparently.

"You need to be nicer to Papa," Sam said.

"He needs not to question what I do for a living. I take it he left?"

Sam nodded as he dried a glass. "He said he'd talk to me later and left."

Disappointment was the first emotion to hit her and that just made her angry. She wanted to yell at Sam but looking at her employer, she knew he was too tired at the moment. This time of year was always hard on him and Joey didn't want to add to that.

"Just two more hours, then we get to close up."

And with that, she went back out into the fray. It was best to just forget her problems and throw herself into work.

By the end of those two hours, she was happy to shut the door and lock it behind the last customer.

"Thank God. I thought they would never go away."

"Hey, we have to pay the bills," Thelma said with a laugh. She'd been out all night talking with customers and helping field the tables. It was great to see her out and about. "Why don't you head home?"

Normally Joey would argue with Thelma. Tonight though, she couldn't find the energy.

"Sounds good. I'll be in early tomorrow."

Christmas Eve. One of the best and worst nights in a bar—with people who would be there to celebrate the season and others who came to drown their sorrows.

After pulling on her coat and grabbing her purse, she headed out to her apartment. She was about halfway home when she felt it. There was a feeling of being watched…followed. Ever since her attack years ago, she was normally very conscious of her surroundings.

Stewart. He was probably there to make sure she made it home okay.

"You can come out now. I know you're there."

She gasped and found the frat boy from earlier standing just a few feet behind her.

"So nice to see you again," he said as he approached her.

CHAPTER EIGHT

Cold, unadulterated fear slithered through Joey's blood. She'd seen that look on a guy's face before. This time, though, it was different. This time, she wouldn't take it.

"I think you need to leave." Her voice sounded stronger than she felt. She knew it was more about perception and not reality though. At least, that's what Sam had taught her when he taught her to fight.

Know your enemy.

Frat boy couldn't hold his liquor. She knew the little bastard was still tipsy. His words were slurring when he spoke. If she was lucky, he went to drink somewhere else.

Lose your baggage.

The memory of those words had her dropping her purse just in case the stupid boy didn't leave.

"Now why would I want to do that? I thought we could share some Christmas cheer."

The idiot kept approaching. He was close enough she could smell the stale beer emanating from him. He smelled as if he had bathed in it. He reached for her with those grubby little hands. Fear and anger surged as she swung her fist in his direction. He caught it, most probably by accident. It also gave her an opening. Joey raised her knee and hit him squarely in the crotch. He screamed and dropped her arm, falling to the ground.

Don't have pity. If they attack you, they deserve it. Don't give the bastard an inch.

He was on his knees, so she punched him. The crack of bone was particularly horrifying and pleasing at the same time. He fell back, blood spurting from his nose and his head hitting the pavement.

"You fucking bitch. You broke my nose."

He apparently had enough beer to allow him to ignore the pain of the broken nose and the kick to his crotch because he was trying to stand again.

Go in for the kill. No mercy until your enemy surrenders.

She knew the one thing men protected more than anything else and she kicked him in the crotch again. This time, he fell into a fetal position. Footsteps sounded behind her. She turned ready to confront who was coming. Relief surged the moment she realized it was Stewart.

He grabbed her by the upper arms and pulled her closer to him. "I thought you would be a little longer or I would have been here to walk you home."

There was a groan from behind her. Stewart looked over her shoulder and she watched as pleasure spread over his features.

"You beat the shit out of him."

She laughed, but she knew it didn't sound right. It sounded…off.

He sighed, kissing her temple, and walked her to her apartment stairs. It was as if she was in a daze.

He walked her up the steps, and unlocked the door for her. She realized he had picked up her purse at some point.

"You sit here," he said, leading her over to the kitchen table. "I'll be right back."

"Stewart," she said as he turned to leave. "Don't kill him."

He looked disappointed.

"Okay."

"I kind of like you. I want to make sure you don't go to jail."

At that, he gave her one of those smiles that usually melted every worry. For some reason, it didn't this time. "Be right back."

* * * *

By the time Papa made it back to the sight of the altercation, college boy was still there. What a dumbass.

He was up on his knees, so Stewart squatted to look the bastard in the eye. Blood was smeared over his face; his nose was definitely going to be crooked. Damn, he loved that woman.

"Shit, son, she really clocked you good."

"I'm going to sue that bitch."

Stewart leaned closer so their faces were only a few inches apart. "First, you're not going to admit to anyone that a girl beat you up."

"She didn't."

Papa shook his head.

"Yeah, she did, or you don't have a case. Of course, if you do sue her or bother her in any way, you might want to run."

"What the fuck does that mean?"

Papa grabbed him by the hair and jerked his head up so that frat boy could see that he meant business.

"See, while you've been safe and cozy here in North Carolina, I've been trained by the United States Marine Corps. Know what I do, dipshit? I'm Special Forces. Know what that means?"

The idiot shook his head.

"That means your parents' tax dollars have paid to teach me how to hunt other men. Hell, I spent six months in a foreign country doing just that. I'm in a unit that specializes in recon. There are other Marines who are afraid of my unit. And you know if the bravest men in the good old U S of A are afraid of us, you should be scared shitless."

He leaned closer so that he was only inches away from the bastard. "There will be no rock big enough to hide your cowardly ass, college boy. And when I find you…well, let's just say dental records are going to be needed to identify your body and your poor mama is going to have to have a closed casket funeral. Understand?"

"Y-yes."

"You get yourself home and hope I don't change my mind and come find you later."

Then, even knowing it was stupid, he pulled back and slammed his fist into the bastard's face. The coward went down, completely passing out from the last hit.

Papa stood up, drew in a deep breath and headed back to Joey's apartment. He wanted to kick his own ass for not getting back to the bar in time. He'd gone out, irritated that she was putting up roadblocks when he was sure he'd made some headway with her the night before. He had planned on being back to walk her to her apartment, but he'd gotten held up by an accident on the road.

Rage still poured through him. He knew he didn't have to hit the bastard at the end. Joey had taken care of herself pretty well, thankfully. He still wanted to hurt something…mainly someone. He'd gotten his punch in though. Now, he had to calm himself before he made it to the top of the stairs that lead to Joey's apartment. He gulped in a few breaths of cold air, then opened the door.

* * * *

Joey tried to keep herself busy until Stewart made it back. She was filling up the teapot when the door opened slowly. Just like earlier that night, she knew who it was without looking. She hated the fact that she was comforted that he was there.

"Are you okay?" he asked softly.

She nodded, trying to hold it together. It would not be like last time. It wasn't. This time, she defended herself. No one would be able to say it was her fault.

Joey felt him approach her, but she didn't hear him. Part of that training he was so proud of.

"Are you sure he didn't hurt you?"

"I didn't give him the opportunity."

"Where did you learn to fight like that?"

"Sam. When I started working there, he said I needed some lessons. I think Thelma told him…"

She realized then how upset she was. She had almost blurted out the one thing she told almost no one. He touched her shoulder and she jerked.

"Sorry."

"No, it just took me by surprise. It's okay."

He slipped his arms around her, and she leaned back into his warmth. "You don't always have to be the strongest person in the room, Joey."

She sighed as she closed her eyes trying to keep the tears from falling. The confrontation had her entire body on alert and, normally, she would shy away from physical contact. With Stewart, it was different. There was something about him that had her yearning for his touch.

"I don't want to be the strongest. I just want to survive."

And that was all she had been thinking about when she started to hit that college kid. He'd touched her and she was back in high school, Jason Pierson's sweaty hands on her and she'd lost it. Right there and then, Joey wasn't sure if she had hit the college kid because of what he had tried or what Jason had done five years earlier.

"Well, you definitely did that. I have little doubt that college boy will remember to respect women after tonight."

She laughed but it ended on a sob.

"Hey, Joey, baby."

His voice was equal parts soothing and panic. It was a strange combination that she would have normally laughed at, but right now, she didn't see a reason to laugh. Stewart turned her his in arms so they faced each other. He pulled her closer and just held her. Joey felt the brush of his mouth against her temple. His heart beat against her ear. He stood there in her apartment and rocked her.

"I…" she couldn't think of anything to say. She shivered as the adrenaline started to fade and she realized how close she had been to going through that experience again.

"Shh," he said. And for once, she listened to a man. She sobbed against Stewart's shirt and again, she didn't know if it was for tonight or for the memories that still bothered her. It didn't really matter. All that mattered was that she was safe, there in Stewart's arms.

After a few moments, he lifted her into his arms and walked her into the alcove where her bed was. He laid her on the bed and Joey expected him to lay down with her.

Instead, he kissed her forehead. The gentle touch had her craving something else, something more from a man. Something she hadn't wanted for five long years. The need had been building the last three weeks. Every time she was with him, the ache for him grew. When she reached for him, he shook his head.

"That wouldn't be right."

Disappointment crashed down on her. She realized he must have figured out what had happened all those years ago and there were men who were disgusted by women who'd been raped.

She sighed, not realizing until now just how much she had needed him to touch her. She was agitated by her own desires and his reaction to them. When she spoke, her voice was harsher than it normally was.

"Then, just go."

He shook his head again. "I'll sleep on the couch. You rest. I'll be here if you need me."

Stewart kissed her on the forehead again, then pulled the sheet she used for privacy closed. She lay back down and stared at the water stained ceiling above her bed. Joey wanted to be mad. She was irritated, but there was comfort in knowing that Stewart was just a few feet from her. It was something new for her. Comfort with a big old bad Marine standing guard.

With that thought, she slipped off her shoes and jeans. At that point, she just decided sleeping in her t-shirt was enough. Moments later, she was snugged in her bed; the horror of the night fading and the contentment of having Stewart close by filled her.

Damn Marine.

It was her last thought before falling asleep.

CHAPTER NINE

Papa woke up before the sun. Years of training couldn't stop that from happening. He was a creature of habit, unfortunately. He sat up and stretched. The cracks that sounded as he twisted his back made him feel old. He knew he was much too young for those kinds of sounds to emanate from his body.

He hadn't had much sleep. Part of it was the couch. He doubted Joey would have been able to fit on it. The other trouble he had was the woman herself.

She hadn't said much about her past, but he had figured out part of it. He knew she didn't trust men. He thought she'd been burned, maybe treated badly by a guy so she avoided them. Now he knew better.

There was no mistaking the terror he'd seen on her face last night as she beat the shit out of the college boy. Even with the situation, he felt his lips twitch. The women packed a hell of a punch and Papa was pretty sure that kid would think twice about taking on a woman again. Hell, with the kick to his crotch, Papa wasn't sure the kid was going to have a fully functioning weapon for a while.

His smile faded as his mind moved back to Joey. He decided not to think too much about the woman. He was a little too raw from the night before and besides, he had morning needs to attend to.

After he was done, he walked out of the tiny bathroom and glanced toward the curtain where Joey slept. As soon as he had closed it the night before, he knew it was more than just to shield herself in the room. It seemed she was cocooned from the world in a way. She participated, but she was always careful about how much she involved other people in her life. Damn, he had to have been stupid not to have picked up on some things. She didn't scare easily. Now that he looked back, there were times that she positioned herself in a place to have a quick escape. She was skittish of men…but not him. Not now. She seemed comfortable around him. Last night, she'd wanted him in her bed. And sadly, he had turned her down.

He sighed. That had been one of the hardest things to do. From the moment he had seen Joey Antonio he had wanted her. It wasn't something he could explain to most people, but he understood the Santini Curse. Most Santini men knew when they met the woman for them. He had mocked it for years. The younger generation always did. Papa hadn't truly believed it until he'd stepped into that bar. Now, he knew what his uncles and father talked about.

In the three weeks he'd known her, she'd not only engaged him on that primal need. Now, she'd crawled right into his heart. He didn't know the entire story behind what had happened to her. Knowing it, knowing what she had built for herself…he couldn't help but fall for a woman like that.

He hadn't paid much attention to the room the night before, but now that he glanced around, he realized just how much Joey was in that room. It was simple, not garish. There were small splashes of color here and there. Then, he saw the paintings. They lined the wall in an area where he assumed most people would put a table for dining. The window on one side probably afforded her the best light to work.

Damn, she was talented. There were landscapes of the beach. Not during the sunny summer. No, this showed the sea rough and the sky overcast. Then he realized that was the way it had looked when they had taken a walk the week before. There were pencil drawings of Sam and Thelma, then he came to the easel. It was covered, but Papa just couldn't resist. He pulled the fabric up and found himself staring back.

He wasn't sure how he felt about it. He had never had someone draw his picture, much less paint him. It was a little odd to see himself on the canvas. Still, he had to admit again, she was damned talented.

And the fact that she had spent time working on him was a good sign in his mind.

"Do you think you have the right to snoop around my apartment?"

* * * *

Joey stood on the opposite side of the room from Stewart and tried to erase the fear that had gripped her just moments ago. The squeak of the floor had pulled her out of a dreamless sleep. Panic hit first, her heartbeat accelerating. Then, she remembered Stewart had spent the night.

Peeking out of the curtain, she had found him nosing around her work and she hadn't liked that one bit. She felt exposed, mainly because no one had really been in her apartment other than Sam and Thelma. Since high school, she'd kept her work to herself.

"I don't see it as snooping. The pictures were out."

"Not that one."

And that is what embarrassed her more than anything. Painting him had been a moment of weakness...a need that had seemed to drive her to do stupid things lately. She really needed to stop that

"Yeah, about that. I'm not sure..." His voice trailed off. He looked at the painting then back to her.

Crossing her arms beneath her breasts, she straightened her spine. "I didn't ask for your opinion."

"It's..." something shifted on his face and his expression cleared. "You only do pictures of people you like."

"So."

Well, that was mature, Joey.

"So, if you're working on a painting of me, that means you like me."

She saw no reason to lie. It would just make her look stupid. But it didn't mean she had to expose herself to him. Laying her emotions bare would only leave her hurting in the end.

"A little bit."

His lips curved, showing her those damned dimples of his, which drove her insane. He was always handsome, but when he smiled at her like that—like she was the only woman in the world—he was deadly. Even knowing that pretty boys didn't always follow through didn't seem to matter. And, last night, well, he wasn't that interested in her. Not now.

"You like me a lot. I mean, it's not just a drawing." He motioned to the stack of papers on the kitchen counter. "No, this took time and effort."

It had. She had tried to ignore it. For the first time in her life, she had tried her best to ignore the need to paint an object. And of course, she had failed. Giving in just that week, she had started on it.

She tightened the cross of her arms. "And?"

He approached her slowly and pulled her into his arms. She kept hers crossed, not wanting to surrender to the need to slip them around his waist. It would be so easy to rest her head on his chest and just ignore the world.

He leaned down and brushed his mouth over hers. Despite her own needs, she didn't respond. Instead, she frowned. He pulled back.

"What's wrong?"

"I don't know what you want from me, Stewart. I really don't."

"What's that supposed to mean? I think I've been pretty open about my feelings from the beginning."

"You have, but last night..."

She didn't want to say he rejected her the night before, although, that's exactly what he did. It was too embarrassing to even admit out loud.

"What? I didn't take advantage of the situation?"

She nodded, feeling her face heat. "Well, not take advantage. You know what I mean."

He pulled back further but he didn't let her go. He slipped his finger under her chin and raised her head so she had no choice but to look at him.

"It would have been taking advantage. And, I'll admit, it would have been much easier to do that. But I know you, better than you think. You would have used last night's incident as an excuse. When you come to bed with me, I want you there because you *want* to be there. Not because you want to escape memories."

She sighed. Damned if he wasn't everything she ever wanted in a man. Honorable, sexy and dammit, he had a sweet streak.

"I thought it was because, well, some guys are put off by that."

"Are you talking about last night, or the thing from your past?"

So, he had figured it out. "Either. Both."

He slipped his hands down her arms. "First, last night, well, it made me happy I'm not a jerk like college boy. Seriously, Joey, there is a good chance the man is still talking with a soprano voice this morning."

Her face flushed and she looked away. "I'm not going to apologize."

"Good."

She glanced back at him.

He nodded. "That's right. You had every right to beat the shit out of him and I am happy you did it."

Then, apparently to prove his point, he cupped her face. When he stroked her cheeks, she felt the calluses there from his work. Without closing his eyes, he dipped his head and pressed his mouth on hers. This time it wasn't just a little peck. This went beyond the few kisses he had given her before.

She let her eyes slide shut and fell into the kiss. Wet, luscious, passionate…there were so many words that would describe the kiss. The one color that came to mind was bright, brilliant red. She felt drenched in it by the time Stewart pulled back. He rested his forward against hers.

"You have to know it was damned tough to walk away last night."

Relief rushed through her. "Yeah?"

He chuckled, but it didn't sound as if he found anything funny. "Yeah.

As in, not sure I had a fully functioning brain when I woke up this morning."

She snorted.

"It's not funny. Marines don't like being shut down, especially when it's the one thing that's been on his mind for weeks."

She tipped her head to the right and studied him. He was telling the truth. From the night he showed up at the bar, it had been like this with him. Most men would have given up long ago, and those turned off by what she had been through would have been gone. Not Stewart.

She shook free of his hands, then cupped his face much as he had hers. Rising to her tiptoes she kissed him. A tickle in her throat warned of the fear that normally gripped her. In the next instant, she brushed it away. This was Stewart and with him she never had to fear anything.

Feeling bolder, she opened her mouth, tracing the seam of his lips with her tongue. He opened his and groaned. He slipped his hands around her waist and pulled her closer. The hard ridge of his penis pressed against her and, again, there was no fear. Instead, that same craving she'd had before, the thing that had driven her to paint the man, took over. Before she was ready though, he pulled back. He drew in deep breaths, gulping at the air like a drowning man.

"If we need to stop this, it has to be now."

Each word was spoken with precision, as if he had to concentrate on them to be able to say them.

She smiled and shook her head. "I don't want to stop."

He looked up at the ceiling and said, "Thank you, Jesus." He bent over and picked her up, lifting her so she was draped over his shoulder.

"Stewart."

He laughed. "You have to give me this, Joey."

He carefully set her on the bed.

"We'll go slow."

She knew then he understood what had happened before. She also realized he was the perfect man to take to her bed for the first time. He would be understanding.

He undid the sash on her robe, laying it open slowly.

"You know you don't have to be so gentle," she said half jokingly.

He shook his head as he cupped her face. Then, he trailed his fingers down her body. She was still wearing her panties and the shirt from the night before.

"I'm not being gentle. I'm savoring this moment. I wasn't sure it would ever happen."

Just hearing that gave her the confidence to lift up and kiss him. The simple touch of her mouth against his drew a shudder from him. Joey pulled back and stared at him. He opened his eyes as his mouth twisted.

"What?"

It took her a moment to come up with the words. "I just never understood."

"That you could be my downfall?"

"No."

"Well, damn, I shouldn't have told you."

She lifted her hand to trace his jaw. "It's a new feeling."

He leaned down and gave her a long, wet kiss. It was her turn to shiver. When he pulled back, his eyes had grown darker.

"How about we destroy each other, baby?" he asked.

She laughed and pulled him back down. This time, he covered her body completely. There was no doubting his arousal as she felt him hard against her belly. Instead of rushing it, he kissed his way down her body, as if savoring the taste of her flesh. He pulled her shirt up, following it with his mouth. He was going too slowly for her. She wanted his wicked tongue on her. Everywhere.

With jerky movements, she worked her shirt over her head and was rewarded as he took one of her nipples into his hot mouth. She had expected to feel apprehension...but there was none. Instead, she wanted to indulge, to be taken over by him...and to take. She wanted to touch and taste like he was. At the moment, Joey couldn't figure out how to move though. He was killing her with every touch of his hands and his mouth.

He kissed his way across her belly. He tugged at her panties and she lifted up to help him. Instead of just falling on her, he rose up to his knees, taking her foot into one of his hands.

"What are you doing?" she asked.

He said nothing. Instead, he kissed her ankle. Heat swelled through her blood, pushing her already burning passion to new heights. There was no fear, no worries for her. Every time she had tried before this, she had been apprehensive. And now she understood. She trusted Stewart. Something in her knew that he would never hurt her on purpose.

He kissed down her leg, pressing her legs open and setting his mouth on her core. The first swipe of his tongue against her and she was lost. Every lick sent her closer to the pinnacle, but not far enough. Soon, she was moving with him, her moans growing louder by the second. She molded her hands to the back of his head, urging him closer. When she thought it would never happen, that she wouldn't reach that end, her world shattered, pleasure rippled through her. She moaned his name, long and loud.

Just moments later she lay completely spent, her body a mass of melted bones. He was already pulling off his clothes, throwing them on the floor behind him. She knew how much he liked order, so it told Joey he was barely thinking of anything else except being naked.

He joined her back on the bed and covered her with his body. Stewart leaned down and kissed her. The passion that he felt was easy to taste, as was the pungent desire from her own body. He entered her slowly then.

Joey was still swollen from her release and he wasn't a small man. She didn't care. There was no panic like every time she tried before this. Now, there was only the pleasure of being connected to him this way. As he started to move, she felt her own needs building again.

"Oh, yeah, that's it, Joey," Stewart groaned, as his thrusts shook her small bed. She barely heard that. She was blind and deaf to everything but the pleasure they were sharing. It didn't take her as long this time to reach orgasm. She came easily, bowing up against him, taking more of his cock inside of her. He thrust two more times, then came, pouring himself into her body.

10 CHAPTER NAME

As they lay in bed listening to the December rain beat against the windows, Papa thought he pretty much had the best Christmas Eve in his recent memory. Joey was tucked in beside him and although the bed was too small for the two of them, neither seemed to care.

It had been several hours like this. They had gotten up and made eggs then ended back in bed making love again. There was one thing that was bugging him though.

As if reading his thoughts, she said, "I'm not sure I can talk about it."

He knew she wasn't speaking of the night before.

"It's up to you."

There was a part of him that completely understood. He had to wait for her to tell him, if ever. She rose up, resting her weight on her elbow.

"It is the defining moment of my life. Until now."

He smiled. "I like hearing that."

"You don't understand. I've tried this before and had not been able to follow through. Now though...to be able to share this has been amazing. I thought I might be frigid. When it happened..."

She swallowed and he knew she was trying to gain the courage to tell him about it. He had to be patient.

"He blamed me. Said I had led him on, that I was the one who was at fault."

He lifted his hand to touch her face. She shook her head.

"No, let me say this. He said it was me who had the problem. I was probably one of those girls who didn't enjoy sex. When I had the problems with guys later...well, even though I understand why he said it, I was worried."

Rage was too simple a word for what he was feeling. "Are you going to tell me his name?"

She snorted. "No. I don't want to be responsible for making you go to jail."

He looked up at her. His surprise must have shown on his face.

"I know you better than you think I do, Stewart. Better than I thought I did."

He leaned up and kissed her. When he pulled back, she smiled, her eyes barely open. "And you know why he doesn't matter tonight? Because of you. You showed me it wasn't me...that it wasn't something I did to lead him on. No, this was all his warped view. And I'm not frigid!"

Satisfaction filled him. "No, you're not."

"In fact," she said, a mysterious smile curving her lips, "I think I have something I have been wanting to do to you."

"Is that so?"

She nodded. Then, she completely surprised him again. She lifted the sheet and started to kiss her way down his body, just as he had done to her. With each touch of her soft lips against his skin, his cock twitched. He was dangerously close to losing control when she settled between his legs.

The expression on her face was of a woman in power, enjoying her ability to take charge. He knew she needed it, needed to take control of the situation. He was going to let her continue as long as he could. Closing his eyes, he surrendered to her. Her breath danced over the tip of his cock the moment before he felt the wet warmth of her tongue. She was inexperienced, but she made up for it by teasing him.

With the flick of her tongue, she almost made him come right there and then. He had never been so undone by a woman. Joey took him fully into her mouth and he slipped his fingers through her silky hair. Closer and closer she pushed him. When she hummed, the vibrations filtered out over his body and he groaned. He'd had enough.

"Come on up here, Joey."

She gave him one last lick and then worked her way back up to his mouth. She kissed him, her tongue dancing against his. Then she moved to the side. He shook his head.

"You're in charge, right now," he said, urging her on top of him. He positioned her just right. He could feel the damp heat of her arousal. "Take me in."

Her eyes widened, then she smiled. Slowly, she lifted up. After taking his cock into her hand, she eased herself down on him. Her rhythm was slow, and it was driving him insane. He didn't interfere, but he did urge her on. Sliding his hand between her legs, he massaged her clit. She shuddered and moaned. Damn, he didn't think he had ever seen anything as beautiful as Joey at that moment. Her hair was a tangled mass of silk as she closed her eyes and leaned her head back.

"Yes," she whispered, in the next instant she came. Her body shuddered with her orgasm. Even in the throes of pleasure, she looked down at him and said, "Stew."

Just the sound of his name on her lips was enough. He thrust up into her one more time and also came. She collapsed on him moments later, the only sounds in the small apartment was their heavy breathing and the rain still battering the window.

* * * *

Papa watched her sleep. It wasn't easy to get a good angle. Her bed was tiny and she was a snuggler. It stunned him to realize he was probably one of the few who knew it.

He wanted to wake her up, but he waited. Her sleep the night before hadn't been all that restful. As if she felt his study, she stirred awake.

Her eyes fluttered, then opened. She smiled up at him. It was the sweetest thing he had ever seen.

"Morning."

He smiled. "Good morning to you."

She glanced over at the clock. "Thank God I don't have to work at the art supply store today."

Joey burrowed closer, her head right over his heart. Right then, he knew without a doubt he would love her until the day he died.

"So, Sam told me the bar is closed on the twenty-sixth and seventh. How about driving up to DC to meet my folks?"

She stilled, then looked up at him. "Why would I do that?"

"I just thought we would…you know."

Now, something close to panic shifted over her face. "Meet the folks?"

"Yeah. They'll want to meet you."

She sat up, unfortunately pulling the sheet up to shield her breasts from his view.

"Why on Earth would they want to do that?"

"Well, I would think if they knew we were serious, they would want to meet you."

"*Serious*?" she screeched as she scrambled out of bed.

"Yes." He was getting mad now. She was acting like he was asking for her first born.

"We just met."

"We haven't just met. We've known each other for a month."

She shook her head. "I don't know you."

"What?"

"I...I barely know you."

"But you slept with me?" He didn't mean to shout at her. She seemed to be pressing some buttons he didn't realize he had.

"I've slept with a lot of men."

"You have not."

"I have too."

He knew she was lying but arguing wasn't going to get him anywhere. "Never mind. We'll talk about it later."

She opened her mouth, but he gave her a warning look. He pulled on his pants, found his shirt and tugged it on. He barely had his shoes on as he stomped out the door and down the stairs. It was Christmas Eve, *dammi*t, and he didn't know where he was going. Without a thought, he made his way back to his apartment. It might be noon, but it was close enough to a holiday to start drinking.

CHAPTER ELEVEN

Joey wasn't asleep when the loud banging started on her door. She wasn't in the mood for another drunk to have lost their way. It happened on holidays a lot. Too drunk to make it back to the car, they wandered the streets. She really needed to move.

"Joey Antonio, why don't I know your name?"

Joey knew the voice, but not the drunken tone. It was three on Christmas morning. Of course, she didn't know if she wanted to deal with a drunk Marine either.

"Joey," Sam said through the door. His voice was pleading. "Open up."

She grabbed her robe, tugging it on as she made her way to the door. Opening it, she found Sam staggering under the weight of Stewart.

"What happened?" she asked.

"He showed up at our house a while ago demanding to know your name. Thelma said he was your mess."

Stewart smiled at her. "Hey, Joey."

She would not be charmed, even if he did look cute in a drunken kind of way. His eyes were barely opened and the lopsided smile he was throwing her way only added to the charm.

"You sure do look pretty. That robe makes your hair bright like the sun. You have the prettiest hair. Doesn't she have the prettiest hair, Sam?"

He ruined the compliment, by burping. She rolled her eyes. "Come on."

They made it to the bed, almost dropping him a couple of times. The man was built like a freaking Mac truck.

He fell on the bed. He laughed, then frowned. "I need to know your name."

He burped again and passed out.

She sighed pressing her fingers against her temples. "I'm sorry about this Sam."

"You should be. No Santini gets this drunk. With those men, it's all about control."

His admonition hurt. He was like a second father to her and knowing she let him down really made her feel bad. "I don't think he's drinking because of me."

Sam settled his hands on his hips. "Don't you give me that, young lady. He shows up at our house begging Thelma to tell him your real name. Then, he goes on and on about spending the night here, you getting attacked...why didn't you say anything when you came in today?"

She tried to follow Sam's train of thought but it wasn't easy.

"I—I…" She couldn't come up with an excuse.

"Thelma was hurt you didn't talk to her about it."

"Stewart was here."

And it was as simple as that. She realized in that instant, having him there had not been humiliating. It had been the best thing that could have happened. And the morning of lovemaking and their talks had been just what she needed.

Dammit. He was what she needed. Everything she needed. She didn't want to have a casual affair with the man. She wanted forever. With babies and stuff.

"Oh, no." She was in love with him.

She looked at the drunken mess on her bed.

Sam nodded. "He's going to feel like shit in the morning." He kissed her on the cheek. "Thelma said dinner's at two."

He started to shuffle away.

"Sam."

He turned to face her. She didn't know what she would have done if she hadn't found Sam and Thelma. They had lifted her up and given her the family she needed to help her heal. It was as if they understood her in a way that her family never would. She loved her parents. They were dedicated to their causes and were disappointed when she didn't want to join them. They never comprehended her needs or her desire for art.

"You know I love you and Thelma, right?"

He smiled. "And we love you. Why do you think Thelma picked you out for the drunken idiot? He loves you too. He might not say it, but no man gets that drunk over a woman he just sort of likes. Not a Santini."

She smiled, her heart filling with joy. "Merry Christmas, Sam."

"Merry Christmas, Josephina."

The door shut behind him and she turned to face the man in her bed. He took up most of it.

It was hard to believe that just a month ago, she had never heard the name Santini or cared about this man. He was a pain in her rear end. Busting into her life, telling her he wanted a serious relationship. Hell, he wanted her to meet his parents. That would lead to meeting her parents, who were none too happy with her living the way she was.

She sighed and sat down on the kitchen chair. There was no doubt about it; the man was going to drive her insane.

* * * *

Papa woke up to explosions. At least it sounded that way to him. He jolted up, opening his eyes, then slamming them shut again.

When did the sun get so fucking bright? He dropped back in bed, his stomach doing somersaults. It felt as if someone was taking a jackhammer to his damned head.

"Gonna spend all day in bed, Santini?"

The sickly sweet tone told him he was at Joey's, but he had no idea how he got there. He opened his eyes again, just barely, and realized he was lying in her bed and she was standing next to it, holding a glass of something disgusting.

"Drink." She held it out to him. His stomach launched a revolt. He fought it back. He took the glass and sipped at it. It wasn't bad, wasn't good, but it didn't make him want to throw up.

"What happened?'

"You drank a lot of liquor and made an ass out of yourself."

She wandered away, back to her easel. She had his painting out. The smell of paint had been what had woken him and made him sick.

He blinked. She was only wearing a long paint-stained white shirt. He had to have the mother of all hangovers, if he just noticed that.

"Wait, you said I made an ass out of myself?"

"Yeah. I don't know who you were with, or what you did, but you showed up at Sam and Thelma's demanding to know my name."

Suddenly it came back him. He had a few drinks, but not enough to get drunk. Unfortunately, his friends showed up and he had a few more. After that it got fuzzy, but he did know he didn't drive.

He had been hurting. And he had felt stupid. He knew with Joey he needed to take his time, let her know just how perfect they were for each other. Instead, he had been so happy, he had rushed things. So, he had decided the best option was to get lost in a bottle of cheap whiskey.

Shit, he hoped he didn't do anything too bad.

"I was demanding to know your name? I know your name."

"I am assuming demanding to know my full name. Sam felt that it was my fault and brought you over here."

He sipped a little bit more of the concoction she gave him. He realized now his stomach was settled enough to try standing. With extreme care, he rose out of bed. The room spun, but not so bad he couldn't concentrate on the woman now painting a background behind him in the picture.

"He felt you were at fault?"

"Yes. He said no Santini ever drinks like that. Then, he said you loved me and he left."

He blinked. "He said what?"

"No wait. First, I told him I loved him. He returned the affection. Oh, and dinner's at two, which is in about an hour, so you better shower." She sniffed in his direction. "You smell."

He blinked again. "Go back. Sam told you I love you?"

"Yes. Well, he said that Thelma and he loved me."

Irritation marched down his spine. He didn't have the patience for her games today. "Dammit, Joey quit doing that."

She turned to face him, an expression of mock innocence on her face. "What?"

"You said he said that I loved you. You know what I mean."

"Yes."

He sighed. "Why did he say that?"

"I didn't ask. He said no man gets that drunk over a woman he kind of likes. Which is kind of stupid because really, Stewart, we had a little tiff, then you got drunk. Not well played."

He was still trying to register that Sam had told her that when she asked, "Don't you want to know my reaction?"

Papa was actually afraid to know. He was ashamed to admit it but after the day before, then getting so damned drunk, he wasn't sure he was up for another rejection.

"Well, I will tell you anyway. I think I love you too."

He blinked. "You said you didn't want to be serious."

It was her turn to sigh, but she didn't look away. "I was scared."

She said it in such a small voice he realized she was ashamed. Which was stupid, but he would get to that later. If what she was saying was true, he could spend the next fifty years proving to her that she was the toughest lady he knew.

"You love me?" he asked.

"I said *I think I love you.*"

"You think?" he asked irritated again.

She gave him a Gallic shrug. "I'm not sure about love. If there's a person in your life who drives you crazy but you can't think of life without them, is that love?"

He smiled. "It must be, because it's how I feel about you."

Without being able to hold back anymore, he grabbed her and pulled her into his arms.

"I love you, Stewart."

He smiled and gave her a smacking kiss on the mouth.

She wrinkled her nose. "Oh, really, Stewart, I might love you, but you do need a shower. You smell like the inside of a whiskey bottle."

He pulled her toward the bathroom. "Wanna scrub my back?"

She smiled and nodded, allowing him to lead her to the shower. "We are going to have to figure out how I will go to art school."

He turned and faced her. "I don't have a ring, or a lot of money, but I will make damned sure you go to art school."

She smiled. "You really are the sweetest man."

He leaned forward for a kiss but she pressed her hand on his chest. "Really, Stewart. Shower, now. And toothpaste, that would be good."

He laughed and started the shower. "And, just for the record, I love you too, Josephina."

* * * *

Present day, Warrenton, VA

Joey woke as the first rays of sunlight tried to fight its way through the blinds. Something tightened around her fingers, causing her to blink then open her eyes. Stewart was looking at her.

"What happened?"

Hearing his voice was one of the most wonderful sounds she had ever heard. It was the only Christmas present she needed.

"You're in the hospital."

He moved his head to look around, then winced.

"Oh, don't move."

For some reason, her vision wavered. She didn't realize until then she was crying.

"Oh, Joey, don't cry, baby."

It had been such a long night, and now that she knew he was safe, she couldn't hold it together anymore.

Stewart's fingers tugged on hers, pulling her out of the seat and he did his best to move over to give her space on the bed. She shook her head.

"You need your rest. I don't want to hurt you."

"There is one thing you should know and that is Papa always gets his way."

She tried to snort, but a sob came out. Just as he always did, he pulled her closer, easing her onto the bed. He kissed the back of neck.

"Now, this is the only kind of medicine a Marine needs."

She smiled and closed her eyes and swallowed. "I thought I lost you."

As soon as she whispered the words, she felt a new rush of pain sharpen in her chest. She pressed her hand between her breasts trying to ease the pain.

"Ah, baby, you know there's no getting rid of me."

In the soft glow of morning light, with the whisper of his breath against her neck, and the sounds of the hospital around them, she drifted off to sleep, content she would kick his ass later.

* * * *

The next day, the knock on the door interrupted an argument about just how pissed she was at Stewart. She saw Leo's face in the small glass window.

"Be nice. The kids are here."

"Woman, you don't need to tell me how to behave."

There was no heat in the comment. For the most part, he had let her rant all day about his accident. Joey figured Stewart saw it as penance.

The door opened and Santinis came streaming into the room. Balloons and flowers filled the small area along with two active babies.

"How did you get past the nurses?" she asked as her boys and their wives crowded the hospital room.

Leo gave her a kiss on the cheek. "We used Gianni. You know he can charm anyone."

MJ came up behind him, baby Anna in her arms. "And we used the newest Santinis, who are just dying to spend some more time with Grandma."

Joey held her arms out. "Gimme."

MJ handed Anna over and Joey settled into her chair. Joey watched as MJ took Serena from Leo and took the chair next to hers. The boys gathered around their father, talking over the injuries and his release the next day. She glanced at their wives. MJ looked as she usually did. No one would have known she'd had a baby not long ago. The other three were at various stages of pregnancy. Each of them glowed with the expectancy of new life. Another group of Santinis to raise. She glanced at Stewart, who was watching her, and they shared a smile.

They had built a good life together and they were ready for the next chapter.

With the sounds of the family around her, Joey sat back with a smile knowing she would be enjoying another Christmas with the man that made her believe in love again.

Meet Melissa Schroeder

Born to an Air Force family at an Army hospital Melissa has always been a little bit screwy. She was further warped by her years of watching Monty Python and her strange family. Her love of romance novels developed after accidentally picking up a Linda Howard book. After becoming hooked, she read close to 300 novels in one year, deciding that romance was her true calling instead of the literary short stories and suspenses she had been writing. Since her first release in 2004, Melissa has had over 30 short stories, novellas and novels released with multiple publishers in a variety of genres and time periods. Those releases include the Harmless series, a best-selling erotic romance series set in Hawaii. A Little Harmless Sex, book 1, was one of the top 100 bestselling Nook Books of 2010.

Since she was a military brat, she vowed never to marry military. Alas, fate always has her way with mortals. Her husband is an Air Force major, and together they have their own military brats, two girls, and two adopted dog daughters, and they live wherever the military sticks them. Which she is sure, will always involve heat and bugs only seen on the Animal Discovery Channel. In her spare time, she reads, complains about bugs, travels, cooks, reads some more, watches her DVD collections of Arrested Development and Seinfeld, and tries to convince her family that she truly is a delicate genius. She has yet to achieve her last goal.

www.melissaschroeder.net
twitter.com/melschroeder
facebook.com/melissaschroederfanpage

And now, enjoy the first chapter from Leonardo, the book that started it all!

The Santinis: Leonardo

The bright sunlight almost blinded Leo Santini the moment he walked into Jeff's hospital room.

"Dammit to hell," he muttered.

"Still a vampire, I see," Jeff said with a chuckle.

Leo squinted at him. "And you're still a sun loving freak from Florida."

As Leo approached the bed, he felt some of his anxiety dissipate. His old boot camp buddy looked better than he expected. After the report he read on Jeff's injuries, Leo hadn't been sure what to expect. Just the fact he wasn't completely medicated meant he was making strides.

"Freak? Please. You're the one who moved to Texas."

He settled in the chair beside the bed. "Please. Not like teaching at Ft Sam was my first choice. Of course, it allows me to see your sorry ass."

Leo glanced around the room. There were four beds but at the moment, only two of them were occupied.

"Smith, this is Leo Santini, an old buddy of mine who is teaching here as a medic. Leo this is Roy Smith."

"Nice to meet you, sir," he said.

"Don't call me sir, I work for a living," Leo said good-naturedly.

"I wonder what Vince would say about that."

Leo stretched out his legs as he thought about his brother who was a Marine Lt Col select.

"Last time I said it to him, he suggested I do something that was anatomically impossible."

Jeff chuckled and closed his eyes. "Santinis never mince words."

"That's definitely true. My mother is ashamed of our manners."

He looked good, almost healthy considering that an IED tried to blow him to hell and back. There were still dark circles under his eyes, but Leo understood that probably had more to do with memories than anything else. "Need me to leave?"

Jeff shook his head and opened his eyes. "I'm resting up for my physical therapy."

Smith laughed.

Jeff frowned in his direction. "That's right. Laugh it up. Me, I have to deal with her today."

"Her?" Leo asked.

"The physical therapist. Johnson. She's...scary."

"That's putting it mildly," Smith said. Leo got a better look at him and realized the soldier was much younger, probably a year or two younger than Leo's youngest brother, Gianni. His red hair and freckles along with the baby face that probably made people think he was younger than he actually was.

"Are you telling me you two are afraid of a woman?"

Jeff laughed. "Spoken like a man who has never been married. But yes, I'm afraid of her. She's tiny, but she's a terror."

"Can't you ask for someone else? It would mean just talking to her commander..."

Leo broke off when the two men started laughing again. They were so loud he doubted either of them would have heard him anyway.

"Yeah, no. That's not going to happen. First of all, she's a civilian. Most of the therapists here are. And, truthfully, I was lucky to get her. She's a battleax but she's the best from what I understand. I just wish she wasn't so mean."

He was going to ask more about the woman, but she'd obviously been eavesdropping.

"So, you brought in someone to bitch to, soldier?"

The voice was strong, southern, and—as the men had said—scary.

He turned expecting to see an older woman built like a Mac truck. Instead, he found a woman who would have been blown away from a hard wind. She was lucky if she hit five-foot-three and she was as tiny as Jeff had said. Small-boned, with long dark hair that she had up in a ponytail, she looked so…well not sweet. Her aquamarine eyes narrowed as she studied Jeff. Her scrubs had some kind of cartoon character on them, but she wasn't smiling. Instead, she settled her petite fists on her waist and frowned.

"Well, are you going to answer me, soldier? Or are you Army guys just too wussy to actually answer a little bitty woman like me."

"You didn't give me a chance," Jeff said.

"Oh, sorry. Forgot what branch of the military you're in. I will allow time for you being slow."

Irritated, Leo rose out of the chair. She looked at him, her gaze traveling the length of him. He ignored the flicker of sensual awareness as she studied him. She had to tip her head back to see his face.

"I think you need to settle down there."

She looked past him to Jeff. "Is he your bodyguard?"

"No, ma'am." Leo heard the amusement in Jeff's voice, but he ignored it.

She looked back at Leo. "I would suggest you take a seat and shut it, soldier. I'm here for Markinson not some overgrown idiot."

He stepped in front of her to stop her. That was a mistake. This close he could see the sprinkle of freckles across the bridge of her cute nose. Her skin wasn't ivory, but golden, as if she spent a lot of time in the sun. Worse, her scent teased his senses. It wasn't anything like perfume, though, just sexy, musky woman.

He shook his head and tried to keep his mind on the problem at hand. "Your attitude needs an adjustment."

She looked up at him. He expected something different than the annoyance he read in her eyes. One perfectly sculpted eyebrow rose.

"Oh, really? Listen, I have two more people to work with today and Markinson here takes the longest because he whines. A lot."

"Aw, come on, Johnson, I don't." Jeff did sound like he was whining but he wasn't about to take the nurse's side in the argument.

"Pftt. You cry more than a cheerleader with a broken fingernail."

Leo was ready to give the woman a piece of his mind but he heard Jeff chuckle. "Santini, you can cool it. Johnson is all bark and no bite."

She looked past Leo again, her attention focusing on Jeff. He could see the slight softening of her gaze. If he hadn't been watching so closely, he would have missed it.

"Don't be lying to these people here or I will make you regret it."

She had lowered her voice, but he heard the change in her tone. It hit him that she was handling Jeff the same way his mother handled him and his brothers.

When she looked back at Leo, her gaze hardened. "Are you going to move, Santini, or do I need to make you cry like a girl, too?"

He wanted to argue with her. She was mean as they said but he realized it might be part of her job. As a medic himself, he understood the position she was in. Sometimes patients needed to be pushed. He nodded and stepped aside.

"Now that the bulldog is going to let me near you I have to say I am ashamed of you. Talking about me behind my back. That's just not right, Markinson."

She motioned behind her and that's when Leo saw the orderly. Leo stepped out of the way and she pulled the curtain closed.

"You didn't have to do that," Jeff said.

"Yeah? What if some sweet little old lady walked by and got a shot of you moving and you showed her some skin. She'd pass out. Can't cause that kind of ruckus."

Leo could tell from her voice she was joking but he knew that she had done it to save his friend the embarrassment of being lifted in front of Leo. His opinion of her went up a notch.

The curtain opened quickly and he found himself face to face with her again. Well, face to chest because she was so much shorter than he was. And in that short minute, he couldn't think. She was looking up at him with those amazing eyes and his brain just stopped functioning. Her mouth opened slightly in surprise and all he could think was that he wanted a taste.

She recovered faster than he did. "Make a hole, Santini."

She barked the order like a drill sergeant. Years of being raised by a Marine and years in the military came raring up and he acted immediately. Once he did, he noticed she let out a slow breath.

"Markinson will be back in about forty five minutes if he isn't too much of a wimp today. Come on," she said and marched out the door.

"You don't have to wait around, Santini," Jeff said. "I'm not that much on company when I get back."

"Do you have any physical therapy tomorrow?"

Jeff chuckled and looked up at the orderly who answered. "No, you can avoid Maryanne tomorrow."

Then, he wheeled Jeff out the door.

"She's not as bad as she seems," Smith said.

Leo nodded, his brain still clouded with the scent of her. What the hell had that been about?

"You need anything?"

Smith smiled and shook his head. "Naw, my mamma lives just outside of San Antonio. She makes sure I have everything I need."

Leo still gave him his cell number and told him to call if there was anything he or Jeff needed. Then, he decided it was time to get back to work. As Leo walked down the hall, his mind went back to the physical therapist. It might seem silly, but he wanted to make sure that she was as good as they said she was. He owed Jeff a lot and he wanted to make sure that he was taken care of. And while his body might be attracted, he couldn't let that get in the way. Jeff was on his own since his divorce. Both his parents were gone and he had been an only child. Someone had to look out for him.

Leo knew he owed the man at least that much for saving his life.

"I know you said he's okay, but I wanted to make sure I didn't push him too hard," Maryanne said into her cell phone as she tried to pull a basket free. The little plastic seat was stuck between two buggies. She jiggled it a few times before giving up and moving onto another one.

"He's fine, MJ," Freddy, her supervisor said. "He's tired, but you did right by him today. He needed to be pushed. He's getting a little lazy. I have a feeling someone has conflicted feelings about going back in the field."

She had seen it too many times to count these past few years—even with her own brothers. She didn't blame any of them for questioning if they wanted to go back in the field, but the truth was, she couldn't have Markinson get too lazy. He wouldn't be able to recover properly from his surgery if he didn't continue to move forward.

"Okay. Well, I'm going to pick up something for dinner here at HEB and then I am going to head home."

"You need a life, girl," Freddy said. "And a social life."

"Don't I know it, but I work for some pain in the ass at BAMC."

"I will ignore that because I love you. I know a great guy I could set you up with."

"I doubt you know a man who would be interested in me, Freddy."

"No, I promise, I have it on good authority that this one is heterosexual."

Freddy was the sweetest gay man with the worst gaydar. The last setup had been with a man who was more flamboyant than Liberace.

"No. No more setups. Call me if you have any issues with Markinson."

She clicked off the phone before Freddy could retaliate with guilt and pushed her way into the grocery store. It was already dark outside and she wanted to get home. She had stayed late to keep an eye on Markinson. Plus, she'd had a lot of paperwork to do. Before she knew it was after eight on a

Friday night. Freddy was right, she thought as she looked around the produce section. She needed a life. She couldn't remember the last time she had a real date, let alone any kind of sex. Maybe that should be her mission for the summer. The mission for booty.

She chuckled to herself. She would settle for a nice night out with an attractive man. If she could find that, Maryanne was pretty sure Freddy would get off her back.

She started going through the oranges and her mind went back to Markinson. He seemed like the perfect soldier but she knew there was something holding him back. If she could figure it out, then she might be able to help him more.

Normally, the first person she would ask would be Santini, but that wasn't an option. The moment she had seen him, her body had reacted. Those wide shoulders, the buzz cut, the bigger than life presence.

She shivered.

From the time she was a teen she had a thing for military men. Military brats often went one way or another. They wanted nothing to do with the military or they were enamored with every sexy military man they could find. She wished she hadn't been in the latter category.

She was not going down that path again. Military men were not for her. Still, when he'd focused those golden brown eyes on her, she had lost all ability to think for a second or two. And that was saying a lot. Hell, she had to fight the urge to fan herself right now thinking about him. All those muscles, that bright smile, and he was tall—at least six feet.

He was in good shape thanks to his job. Markinson had told her Santini was a medic he had served with in Iraq, and that definitely showed in those massive arms. She shivered. They were the kinds of arms that made a woman feel safe.

No. No. No!

She had too many military men in her life. Her father was a marine, her brothers were all marines, and she worked daily with military men. She knew the only thing that would come out of any kind of attraction was heartbreak. It wasn't like he was going to ask her out. From his reaction to her, he probably would have some kind of background check done on her. Not that he would find anything.

She put the bag of oranges in her cart, turning she ran smack dab into a man.

"Whoa, there, Ms. Johnson."

Dammit, she knew that voice. She would probably think about it when she was...never mind thinking about that.

She tipped her head back and found Santini smiling down at her.

"Do you always run around like you're hell bent for leather?" His lips curved into a lopsided smile that had her brain shutting down. "Cat got your tongue?"

She shook her head and tried to step back. It was then that she realized he had those massive hands wrapped around her forearms. His thumbs were caressing her skin ever so slightly. This close she could smell the fresh clean scent of him. All soap and hard, sexy man.

Mother help me.

He looked down at his hands then back up at her. "Oh, sorry. Wanted to make sure you didn't fall down."

He hesitated then released her.

She studied him realizing that he hadn't changed out of his BDUs.

"What are you doing here?" she asked.

"Shopping?" he said with amusement as he tipped his head toward his buggy. She eyed all the fruits and vegetables.

"That's a lot of food for one guy."

He crossed his arms over his chest and she tried to ignore the way his pecs flexed—but she failed. She swallowed—hard—and forced her attention from them to his face.

"I like to eat."

She rolled her eyes and turned to leave. She needed to get away—far away—from the temptation of Santini. If she were lucky he would leave her alone. His footsteps behind her told her she wasn't so lucky.

She stopped and he almost ran his cart into her. With a sigh she turned to face him.

"What?"

His eyes widened and she realized that she had raised her voice. A glance around the department told her she had gained the attention of the few people shopping that late at night.

Maryanne slipped around his buggy. "I thought guys like you only shopped on post."

Something that looked like guilt moved over his face before he hid it. Great, now he was coming up with a lie and they weren't even involved. What the hell was wrong with her? This is what she found attractive. The perfectly nice accountant she had dated a few months earlier never lied to her but she just lost interest, mainly because he was perfectly boring.

"I had some work, which I'm sure you did too?" he said, his smile returning.

She did not want him smiling at her. She needed him pissed at her, being mean to her, and staying away from her. When he was smiling like that it just made her want to scream. And kiss him. She really, really wanted to kiss him.

"And you decided to drive all the way over here to Universal City to shop at the HEB? Isn't there one closer to post?"

He nodded. "This one is closer to my apartment."

Oh, so not good.

"Don't tell me you live at the Live Oak Apartments."

"I sure do. Just moved in two weeks ago."

She narrowed her eyes as she studied him. Growing up as the only sister of three older brothers made her very good at detecting bullshit.

He seemed to be telling the truth, but there was that moment before that made her nervous. Worse, she wanted to believe him. Wanted to have him living near her so she could flirt with him, maybe kiss him...

Dammit.

She had no other choice than to chase him away.

"Listen, this might work with a lot of other women, but I don't like stalkers." She practically yelled it. He wore no expression on his face so she decided to get out before he could retort. Grabbing her cart, she hurried away.

Damn, she really did need to get a life.

Leonardo is sold as an individual title everywhere in digital and in the Santinis Collection in both print and digital.

The wildly successful Santinis resulted in the spinoff series: Semper Fi Marines. The first book, Tease Me, is now available in print and digital from retailers everywhere!

TEASE ME

A man who thinks he has what he wants.

Bran Johnson always knew he wanted to be a Marine. What makes it even better is longtime gal pal TK is now stationed at the same base. Unfortunately, Bran is having a hard time dealing with his feelings when he realizes that TK is considered a hot commodity on base. Worse, he finds himself taking a backseat to her admirers.

A woman who always wished for more.

Tess Keller has loved Bran since they were in high school. The former football captain always treated her like a friend so she tried to move on. Unfortunately, he's in her business constantly now. One passionate argument leads to more than either of them expected. Tess knows it isn't going to last because Bran is never going to settle down. So, to save face, she suggests they stay friends, only with the side benefit of being sometime lovers.

A Marine determined to win at all costs.

Bran agrees to the friends with benefits idea just to keep himself close to Tess. She might think he's not around for the long haul, but this is one Johnson brother who knows exactly what he wants…and just how to get it. And what he wants is Tess in his bed and in his life forever. Nothing will stop him, not even Tess herself.

And now, please enjoy the first chapter of Tease Me:

Bran Johnson spotted the golden halo of short curls first. It was always easy to find his best friend from high school by her hair. Not many people had that shade of blonde—not naturally. She was walking down the path in front of the Camp Lejeune Naval Hospital heading to the parking lot and she wore scrubs.

He slowed his Camaro and wound down the window. "Hey, there, good looking."

As she glanced at him, Bran had the pleasure of watching her expression change from irritation to complete happiness. Her dimples appeared and joy lit her green eyes.

She jogged over to him. Bran was delighted that she still had the sprinkle of freckles dancing over the bridge of her nose. "Hey, yourself. When did you get here? I thought you weren't due in for another week."

He shrugged. "I had enough of family life in DC for awhile."

She nodded. If there was one person in the world who knew about how his family worked, it was Tess. Time with the Johnsons was fun, but exhausting—especially when spending time with The General.

She leaned back and looked at his convertible. The little humming noise she made caused him to itch from the inside out.

"So, this is the new car?"

In high school, she'd been one of the few girls who appreciated cars. Of course, her father's hobby had been rebuilding old cars, and she'd been his constant companion.

"Come on, I'll take you for a ride."

She didn't hesitate and jumped right in.

"Nice to see you pilots still know how to waste money."

He sighed as he shifted the car into gear. "You always give me shit about my cars and I know it's because you secretly envy them."

"No. I wouldn't be able to deal with something so low to the ground. Give me my Silverado any day."

"So where were you off to so fast?"

"Lunch. I thought I'd run over to the exchange and grab a bite to eat. Needed to get out of the hospital for a bit."

"Sounds good," he said.

"Excuse me, but I don't think I invited you."

He laughed. "Okay, Tess. Can I please come to the exchange with you to partake in lunch?"

She chuckled and he felt a funny shift in his chest. It had been like that the last few weeks as he'd PCS'd from one base to the other. Any time he talked to Tess on the phone, he'd had odd feelings. He'd written it off as nerves about the new job, but it didn't explain why his palms were sweating.

"Okay, since you are new in town and well, I know you can't get a woman. Plus, I'll be happy to let you pay."

"Did anyone ever tell you, you're rude?"

"Yep. But I ignored him. He doesn't count."

"Who called you rude?"

"Your brother, Jack. He said, 'You don't act like a girl. You're rude.' Then I told him to suck it."

"When was this?" He asked.

She motioned with her hand. "Take the next right. This was in high school. None of you knew how to handle a girl who didn't faint at the sight of your pretty faces. Well, Jesse could to a point, but you and Jack couldn't."

He pulled into a parking space and turned the car off. "We became best friends."

"Yes, but not before I gave you a bloody nose."

"That is another example of being rude."

She looked at him, her eyes dancing with humor. "Well, Johnson, don't ever tell a girl she can't punch like a guy. There's a good chance she'll have to prove you wrong."

With that, she slipped out of the car, her laughter filtering back to him. He smiled. Yep, it was good to be stationed there with Tess.

* * * *

They were eating lunch when Tess asked, "So, did you find a place to live?"

He shook his head. She curled her fingers into the palm of her hands to resist brushing back the small lock of hair that fell forward. It was a sure sign he was in need of a haircut.

"I've got a few leads from that realtor you put me in contact with."

Then he smiled at her. Even ignoring the way her pulse skipped, she knew what was coming. He'd used that smile on every girl in school when he wanted something—and not just sex. The boy could charm a nun into participating in an armed robbery. She couldn't handle him in her house. That was too much to ask of her. Plus, she couldn't afford the amount of food he ate.

"No."

He tilted his head. "Come on, Tessy. You have a three bedroom house."

"And you have a pilot's pay and TLA, Dislocation Allowance and per diem." Every time someone PCS'd, they were given extra money to help with the move and for a single guy, it was more than enough to pay for things. "I don't need you in my way."

He opened his mouth to say something when Jed Sawyer stopped by the table.

"Hey, Tess. I didn't know you were working today."

Jed was a nice guy and she had gone out with him several times in the last couple of months. He was infantry and it showed in his build. He was just at six feet tall and Tess was sure he would top the scales at two-thirty—most of it muscle. He had chocolate brown eyes, wavy blond hair and a very talented mouth. Lord, the man could kiss and it had been one of the reasons she'd agreed to another date. In fact, they had a date that night.

She smiled at him. "Jed. Yeah, I wasn't supposed to work, but I traded shifts with someone. Her little boy has the stomach flu and her husband's deployed."

He glanced in Bran's direction then back at her. "Oh, Bran, this is Jed Sawyer. Jed, this is that old friend I told you about, Brandon Johnson."

Something close to relief moved over Jed's face. "Ah, nice to meet you."

Bran nodded, but said nothing. Very strange for him, especially since they were going to be in the same battalion.

Tess noticed Jed was holding a tray filled with food.

"Why don't you join us?" she asked.

Jed shook his head. "I'm eating with Reynolds and Gonzales," he said, motioning to a table. She turned around, smiled and waved at the guys.

"Okay."

"Still on for six tonight?"

"Of course." When he left, Tess turned around to find Bran frowning at her. "What?"

"I just thought we could do something tonight," he said, sounding a little put out.

Oh, and Prince Brandon didn't like having his plans ruined. "Sorry. I made that date last week, not breaking it."

"Oh."

And because they had been friends for almost ten years, she gave in. "Okay. You can stay with me; on the condition you mind your own business. Oh, and you have to buy food. I can't afford to feed you. And, no women. You want sex, you go somewhere else."

"Do you think all I do is eat and have sex?"

She laughed. "Brandon Johnson, I was your best friend in high school. I know that's all you think about." She took another sip of her tea. "Oh, and you are in charge of cleaning up your bathroom. I am *not* going to do it. Men are disgusting."

* * * *

"So, that's the tour of the place."

Bran looked around, thinking he would have been able to tell anyone this was Tess' house. Mainly because it was in order. She liked everything in its place, and that was something he understood. It wasn't part of being in the military. It was more about being a military brat.

Both of them had been born and bred into the military. Government issue. And for a woman, she had very few knick-knacks around the house. Mostly there were pictures of her, her family, along with some with his family.

"I need to get cleaned up and ready for tonight. I would say make yourself at home, but I know you will without the invitation."

He smiled at her. "Sure thing. I guess I can survive."

She rolled her eyes and left him to get ready. It was nice to be back with Tess again. They had been thick as thieves through high school and most of their time at Annapolis. It had been difficult to keep in touch these days. He'd been deployed, as she had, and they both had demanding jobs when they were stateside. Now though, it seemed they were going to have time together and that would be fun.

As he wandered around the living room, his phone rang. *Jesse.*

"Hey, bro, checking up on me?"

Jesse chuckled. "Well, you did say you would call when you got there."

He had, then he'd seen Tess and forgotten all about calling his family.

"I had to secure quarters."

There was a beat of silence. "Don't tell me you're mooching off Tess."

"I am, although she seems too busy to care." And it still pissed him off. It irritated him more that he didn't have a right to be angry about the date. He wouldn't have expected a male friend to break a date to spend time with him, but for some reason, he felt betrayed that she wouldn't dump a guy for him. It wasn't like she was going to marry the guy.

"What's that supposed to mean?"

"She has a date tonight she refused to break."

Another beat of silence. "You expected her to drop a date because you showed up? Did you give her any advanced notice?"

"No."

And Bran knew he was being an ass about it, but he was kind of disappointed that Tess was busy. They hadn't spent any time together since…well since they both graduated from Annapolis.

"I can see where she would have her hands full there."

His tone rubbed on a nerve Bran didn't know he had. "What's that supposed to mean?"

"Come on, Bran. There aren't that many women on base like her, you know that. She's hot."

The nerve was now beyond irritated. "And just when did you see her last?"

Now that he thought about it, the girl with the huge green eyes had grown into her long legs. Those sharp angles had turned into subtle curves and with her hair somewhat tamed, she sort of…well, any other guy would say she stole his breath away.

"I was down there…well, about six months ago. I knew she was stationed there so I called her up and we had lunch."

Bran pulled the phone away from his ear to look at it, then set it against his ear again.

"You had a date with Tess?"

"Good God, no. I can't because, well, she's like a little sister."

Bran snorted. "A little sister you find hot?"

"Couldn't help noticing."

"At least she made time for you."

"I called her ahead of time because I didn't presume. I know she's a single woman on a military base. The fact that she's sweet and good looking, well that adds to the package."

"Sweet?" he asked as he heard a sound behind him. He turned and every drop of moisture in his mouth dried up. Lord. Tess wore a pair of jeans, the type that hugged a woman's hips, and a t-shirt that just barely touched the waistband. When she moved, he could see her belly button and good God, a belly ring. Her hair was a sexy mess of curls as if she had just gotten out of bed.

"Bran? Are you there?"

Bran shook his head trying to get his brain to work again. "Uh, yeah. Just tired from the drive down."

"Okay. Well, I'll tell the old man you're there and MJ, before she calls again."

"She didn't call me."

"She texted you. So you better text her back or the soon-to-be momma to be is going to be upset with you."

He nodded and hung up without saying goodbye.

Tess smiled at him, making his pulse dance. "Let me guess, that was Jesse."

She knew his family well. "Yeah. I forgot to call."

She shook her head. "You know, I'm amazed they let you fly a Raptor. I would think you might forget where you parked it."

He knew she was trying to lighten the mood. That was what he would have done in the situation, but his brain wouldn't work. In fact, he was feeling a little lightheaded but it might have to do with the lack of sleep. It definitely had nothing to do with that belly ring, or his need to see what other interesting things he could uncover on her body.

"You're wearing makeup." It came out as an accusation, but he couldn't help it. He wasn't used to seeing Tess Keller all made up. She wasn't wearing much, but even as he said it, she slathered on lip-gloss. How did he not notice her lips were so full and sexy before now?

She smirked at him. "Yes, I do that sometimes. It's kind of something I do on dates."

"You wear makeup."

"Uh, yeah among other things." She rolled her eyes, a sure sign of

irritation.
He frowned and opened his mouth to ask her just what those other things were, but the doorbell rang.

"There's Jed." She walked to him and gave him a pat his cheek. "Don't wait up."

"Don't you have duty in the morning?"

She stopped with her hand on the doorknob. "First of all, I'm an adult and a lieutenant in the Navy, so I can decide for myself. But, to ease your mind, I'm off tomorrow."

She left him standing there in the middle of the room, mildly frustrated and trying to figure out what the hell just happened.

Infatuation: A Little Harmless Military Romance

To prove her love and save her man, she has to go above and beyond the call of duty.

SEAL Francis McKade never acted on his feelings for his best friend's sister. All that changes at a wedding in Hawaii, but the next morning, he's called for a mission-one that leaves his world in shambles.

Months later, Kade shows up in her bar a changed man. When he pushes her to her limits in the bedroom, Shannon refuses to back down. One way or another, he'll learn there is no walking away from love—not while she still has breath in her body.

Warning: This book contains two infatuated lovers, a hardheaded military man, a determined woman, some old friends, and a little taste of New Orleans. As always, ice water is suggested while reading. It might be the first military Harmless book, but the only thing that has changed is how hot our hero looks in his uniform—not to mention out of it.

The sound of Hawaiian music drifted lightly through the air as Kade took a small sip of his beer. He stood on the side of the dance floor watching the wedding guests. It was one of those days Hawaiians took for granted he was sure, but Kade didn't. The sweet scent of plumeria tickled his nose, and the sound of the ocean just a few hundred yards away combined with the music to ensure that the entire day seemed magical. The groom, Chris Dupree, smiled like a man who had just finished Hell Week with honors, while his new bride, Cynthia, glowed with more than that "happily just married" glow. Her gently rounded tummy was barely visible, but everyone knew she was pregnant.

"Never thought he would settle down," Malachi, Chris' brother, said from beside him. One of Kade's best friends, Mal had dragged him across the Pacific Ocean to make the wedding.

"Really? He's been with her for years. It only took him this long to convince her to marry, right?"

Mal laughed and took a long drink out of his bottle.

"Ain't that the truth," Mal said, New Orleans threading his voice. Their friendship was an odd one, that was for sure. Mal had grown up as part of a huge family in New Orleans, and was half creole. The name Dupree meant something in circles down there, especially in hospitality. Francis McKade grew up the child of Australian immigrants, both scientists recruited to work for the US Military.

"At least there are lots of lovely ladies here for the picking," Mal said, his gaze roaming over the crowd. "There's something about Hawaiian women, you know?"

Kade said nothing but nodded. He wasn't particularly interested in most of the women today. The woman he wanted set off signs of being interested in him, but she had never acted on it.

"Are you two flipping a coin to see who gets what woman?"

The amused female voice slipped down his spine and into his blood. Before turning around, he knew who she was. Shannon Dupree, youngest sister of his best friend, and the woman who had starred in most of his most vivid sex dreams. He turned to face her, thinking he was ready for the impact, but of course he wasn't. As usual, she stole his breath away.

She was dressed in red, the main color of the wedding. The soft material draped over her generous curves. Shannon was built like Kade loved his women. Full hips, abundant breasts, and so many curves his fingers itched to explore. Every time he was near her, he had to count backwards from ten and imagine that he was taking a shower in freezing water. Sometimes that worked.

"What makes you think we're doing that?" Mal asked.

One eyebrow rose as she studied her brother. "I've known you for twenty-eight years, that's how I know."

Shannon turned to Kade expectantly, and he couldn't think. Every damned thought vaporized. It was those eyes. Green with a hint of brown, they were so unusual, and they stood out against her light brown skin. He could just imagine how they would look filled with heat and lust.

He finally cleared his throat and mentally gave himself a shake. Staring at her like a fifteen-year-old with a crush wasn't really cool. "Don't lump me in with your brother, here. He doesn't have any standards."

"Except for that stripper last time you visited?"

There was a beat of silence. "Stripper?"

"Mal ratted you out."

He gave his friend a nasty look. His last visit to New Orleans hadn't gone that well. Shannon had gotten very serious about her current boyfriend, and there had been talk of them moving in together. Kade had done the one thing he could to ignore the pain. He got drunk and went out to strip clubs. And Mal had been the one with the stripper, not him.

"I think your brother had that wrong."

She glanced back and forth between them. "Whatever. Just make sure you stick around for some of the reception before you go sniffing any women."

"Don't worry about me. Your brother has the impulse control problem."

Shannon laughed.

Mal grunted. "Both of you suck."

"They're going to be cutting the cake soon, so at least hold off until then, could you?"

With that she brushed past them, and he could smell her. God, she was exotic. Even with all the scents of Hawaii surrounding him, hers stood out. Spicy, sweet...

He took another pull from his longneck bottle, trying to

cool his libido.

"So, who do you have in mind?" Mal asked, pulling him from his thoughts.

"What?"

"Man, it's a wedding. Women are always ripe for seduction at these things. You have to have someone in mind."

His gaze traveled back to Shannon. She walked through the crowd, her hips swaying sensually as she moved from person to person. Her smile enticed everyone she spoke to. As the owner of a bar and grill in New Orleans, she knew how to work a room. And dammit, she had that perfect smile that drew every man to her. His hand started to hurt, and he looked down to find his fist clenched so tight around his bottle his knuckles were white. It took a couple of seconds to calm himself down. He didn't have a right to be jealous. She wasn't his to love, to protect. He'd learned a long time ago that being a Seal and being married just didn't work out.

He noticed Mal looking at him, expecting an answer.

"Not sure, mate, but I have a feeling I'll find someone to occupy my time."

.....

Shannon shivered as she took a sip of champagne. She tried not to wince at the taste. What the holy hell was she doing drinking it? She hated the drink. What she needed was two fingers of whiskey. It would clear her head of the sexy Seal that had her pulse skipping.

"What are you doing drinking that?" her sister, Jocelyn, asked.

When Shannon turned, she couldn't fight the smile. Seeing the transformation of her sister in the last year was amazing. Seeing her happily married with Kai added to the joy she felt for Jocelyn. Even if there was a little jolt of envy, Shannon couldn't begrudge her the happiness. After the things she had overcome, Jocelyn deserved it more than anyone she knew.

"I thought it best. You know with the jet lag and all that, I need to keep my wits about me. Champagne should help, right?"

Her sister's eyes danced with barely suppressed amusement. "It couldn't be because of one hot Seal with a hint of an Aussie accent, could it?

Shannon closed her eyes and sighed. "That man gets my temperature up. All he has to do is smile, and I'm ready to strip naked and jump his bones." She opened her eyes. "Is it that obvious?"

Jocelyn shook her head. "Just to someone who knows you like I do."

And no two people knew each other better. As the two girls in a huge family of men, they had depended on each other. Only fifteen months apart in age, they were more like twins than just sisters.

“Are you talking about that hot Seal your brother brought with him?” May Aiona Chambers asked as she stepped up to the two women. After meeting her just months earlier at Jocelyn’s wedding, Shannon had instantly liked the sassy Hawaiian. Petite with the most amazing long hair and blue green eyes, she never seemed to have a problem voicing her opinion.

“Oh, May, please, could you join us in the conversation,” Jocelyn said with a laugh.

“As my sister-in-law, you should be used to it by now.” She dismissed Jocelyn and honed in on Shannon. "He’s been watching you.”

“What?” she asked, her voice squeaking. “No he hasn’t.”

“That Seal, he’s been watching you all day.”

Shannon snorted, trying to hide the way her heart rate jumped. "You’re insane. Does this run in the family? You might want to adopt children, Jocelyn.”

“No, really, he has. He does it when he thinks you aren’t looking.”

She turned around and found him easily on the other side of the dance floor. That erect posture made it easy. He always looked like he was standing at attention. Even in civvies, he looked like a Seal. The Hawaiian print polo shirt hugged his shoulders and was tucked neatly into his khaki dress slacks. He wasn't the tallest man in the room, but he stood out. All that hard muscle, not to mention the blond hair and the to-die-for blue eyes, made him a gorgeous package. Everything in her yearned, wanted. Of course, he wasn't looking at them. His attention was on the other side of the room. Probably on some damned stripper. Shannon turned back to her sister and May.

"Are you drunk?" Shannon asked.

May rolled her eyes. "No, really he has. You know what those Seals are like. He can do surveillance without you knowing. It's his job. But you should see the way he looks at you."

She couldn't help herself. "Like how?"

May hummed. "Like he wants to take a big, long bite out of you."

She couldn't stop the shiver that slinked down her spine or the way her body heated at the thought. Since she had met him five years earlier, she had been interested in him. He was quiet, unlike her brothers, and the way he moved...God, she knew for sure he was good in bed. But it was more than that. Kade was sexy, that was for sure, but there was something more to him than just a good-looking man. There was an innate goodness in him, one that made a woman know he would take care of her no matter what.

"If I were you, I would make use of the event to get him in bed."

Shannon snorted again, trying to keep herself from imagining it—and failing. "Please, May, tell me what you really think."

"Believe me, I know about waiting, and it isn't worth it. I waited years for some idiot to notice me. I think of all the time we wasted dancing around like that."

"Did you just call your husband an idiot?" Jocelyn asked.

May rolled her eyes. "He overlooked me for years, then waited forever once he did notice me. Of course he's an idiot. But in this situation, you have to be strategic. I saw Evan almost every day. This guy, he's going to be gone again with that job of his. You have got to take advantage of the wedding and get him into bed. Get a little wedding booty."

She should be mad, but it was hard to be. May looked so innocent with her sweet smile, and her voice sounded like something out of a movie. Shannon just couldn't get irritated with her. Before May could say anything else, they announced the cutting of the cake. She turned to face the banquet table, and as she did, she caught Kade looking at her. It was the briefest moment, just a second, but even across all that space, she saw the heat, the longing, and felt it build inside of her. Her breath backed up in her lungs. In that next instant, he looked away.

It took all her power to turn her attention back to the event at hand, seeing her brother and her sister-in-law staring at each other, she took another sip of champagne. May was right. She had to take a chance. If he said no, if he ignored her, then she could drink herself in a stupor and have months before she had to face him again.

But there was one thing Shannon Michele Dupree did right, and that was being bold. She chugged the rest of her champagne, set it on the table next to her, and headed off in Kade's direction.

That man wouldn't know what hit him.

Other Books by Melissa Schroeder

Harmless

A Little Harmless Sex
A Little Harmless Pleasure
A Little Harmless Obsession
A Little Harmless Lie
A Little Harmless Addiction
A Little Harmless Submission
A Little Harmless Fascination
A Little Harmless Fantasy
A Little Harmless Ride

A Little Harmless Military Romance

Infatuation
Possession
Surrender

The Harmless Shorts

Prelude to a Fantasy

The Santinis
Leonardo
Marco
Gianni
Vicente
The Santinis Collection

Semper Fi Marines
Tease Me

By Blood

Desire by Blood

Once Upon An Accident

The Accidental Countess
Lessons in Seduction
The Spy Who Loved Me

Leather and Lace

The Seduction of Widow McEwan
Leather and Lace—Print anthology

Texas Temptations

Conquering India
Delilah's Downfall

Hawaiian Holidays

Mele Kalikimaka, Baby
Sex on the Beach
Getting Lei'd

Bounty Hunters, Inc

For Love or Honor
Sinner's Delight

The Sweet Shoppe

Turning Paige
Cowboy Up
Tempting Prudence

Connected Books

Seducing the Saint
Hunting Mila
Saints and Sinners—print of both books

The Hired Hand
Hands on Training

Cancer Anthology
Water—print

Stand Alone Books

The Last Detail
Her Mother's Killer
A Calculated Seduction
Telepathic Cravings

Coming Soon

Only For Him-A FREE Harmless Serial on MelissaSchroeder.net (December)
Angus: The Cursed Clan
Semper Fi: Tempt Me
Semper Fi: Touch Me

CPSIA information can be obtained at www.ICGtesting.com
Printed in the USA
LVOW13s1714060714

393076LV00005B/837/P